The Jazz Age Murders

The Jazz Age Murders

a novel by
Kathleen Anne Fleming

CREATIVE ARTS BOOK COMPANY
Berkeley •1999

For information contact:
Creative Arts Book Company
833 Bancroft Way
Berkeley, California 94710

The Jazz Age Murders is published by Donald S. Ellis
and is distributed by Creative Arts Book Company.

The characters, places, incidents and situations
in this book are imaginary and have no relation
to any person, place or actual happening.

ISBN 0-88739-203-2 Paper
Library of Congress Catalog Number 97-78452
Printed in the United States of America

To my husband, John Terzis,
my children, Clare and Nicholas;
and in memory of both my father,
Stanley Baker Fleming,
and my mother,
Rachel Lucinda Fleming.

The Jazz Age Murders

Chapter One

Entering the jazz club another presence overtook her, another world she hadn't seen since the green lawns of suburbia had seduced her away from the gritty enticements of the city. Her husband Jack waited in line outside for their friends Tony and Susan, watching several post-college-aged women sporting asymmetrical hairdos and layers of black lace and spandex. Behind him a young couple kissed sloppily, then lit each other's cigarettes.

Minutes later, the line scattered when a fight broke out between two women wearing leopard skin and leather. Jack stepped back and squinted at the sign over the door of the pub that read "Cleary's Jazz Club." It creaked back and forth in the chilly breeze of a Chicago autumn. Glenda came out and raced over to him.

"I got us a table in the back. It's all they had left — it's packed in there."

"Some place," Jack said. "This Leo Cleary had better be as good as you say."

"The best. Everyone in the music school crowd hits Cleary's. It's part of the Lincoln Avenue night out."

"So why am I fighting this line waiting for the infamous Tony and Susan?"

Glenda searched the line, preoccupied. Suddenly someone threw his arms around her from behind and kissed her neck. She spun around.

"Tony!" she cried, her heart pounding. "Where's Susan?"

"She's inside. Got us a table right in front. You must hear the master Cleary up close."

Glenda nodded. "Meet my husband," she said, turning to introduce Jack.

Jack shook Tony's hand, studying the dark-eyed, swarthy young man. Then he and Glenda followed Tony inside past imposing bouncers. Inside, the smoke and haze closed in. The cool fall night was cut off at the door. Lights dimmed as the pair followed Glenda's dark young friend.

To the right as they approached the small stage, she noticed a black player piano and was reminded of one belonging to her Uncle Max and Aunt Nellie. It had been the center of their living room for decades. She recalled now, in the smoke-filled din of this nightclub, how Aunt Nellie would change the rolls on the piano while Glenda sat mesmerized by the magic of the black and white keys as they magically danced out their tunes by themselves.

As soon as they'd sat down, Susan swaggered up. It was obvious that she had had a lot to drink. Glenda had prayed enough for Susan's recovery. But tonight would clearly be yet another festive evening with more festive drinking. If it had been the crash of 1929, Susan would have used it as an excuse to drink. Susan loved parties. Susan also loved tragedies, people, and crowded nightclubs. Cleary's had been a favorite spot since the two young women had spent their summers waitressing in the area while on break from the University of Illinois in Champaign. Susan's eyes lit up when she saw Glenda, who felt a pang of guilt for despising Susan's alcoholism. Susan rushed forward with her arms out, spilling several drops of her drink.

"Glenda doll, I've missed you. Where have you been?" she said, giving her a hug. "We're so glad you made it!"

Tony stood behind her, frowning. Several young men in leather strode past and he studied their earrings and long hair. Glenda had met Tony many times yet she'd never been sure about his motives. Now she felt her uncertainty may have been valid.

Susan leaned close to Glenda's ear. "Come with me my friend," she said too loudly. "I want to show you something just sickening."

Glenda followed Susan then, weaving through tables. She noticed her friend wore dangling cameo earrings.

"I like your earrings. They're unique."

Susan grinned. "Thanks," she said simply.

Soon they squeezed through a small curtained passageway backstage, passing lackadaisical music lovers in torn jeans and sweatshirts.

"Back here," Susan directed, stumbling into a room tucked around a corner.

Glenda walked into the dimly lit room. In one corner stood a striking young man with curly brown hair and a beard, a reed soaking in his mouth. He watched three young women in mini skirts passing his soprano saxophone from one to the next, testing out his horn using reeds from a nearby cup of water.

"That's Leo Cleary and those are his loyal groupies," Susan said, sarcastically. "They're like alley cats, aren't they?"

"He lets them try out his saxophone? Doesn't he worry someone will break it?"

"Well," Susan said, slurping her drink. "He has a spare sax and a cup full of reeds as you can see. Besides, I think the sexual high these women give his ego is worth a broken reed or two. I'll admit. I too tried out his sax earlier tonight."

Glenda watched the young women.

"Come on," Susan said suddenly, grabbing Glenda's arm. "Tony will wonder where I am. He's a jealous son of a bitch."

Minutes later, Susan plopped down in a seat next to Glenda and handed her empty glass to Tony over her shoulder. He dutifully headed toward the bar.

"Ready for the show?" Susan asked, putting her arm on the back of Glenda's chair.

"I've heard great stuff about Cleary, especially from other musicians."

"Right," she said, rocking back and forth in her chair. "He's an incredible artist."

As she finished, she frowned suddenly.

"What is it?"

Her eyes looked glazed, distant.

"I just don't want to be alone when it happens again."

Before Glenda could speak, Tony returned with the drinks. He set them down slowly, studying Susan's expression.

"What have you told her now?" he asked sternly.

"Don't worry, I won't blow your venture."

Glenda stirred her iced tea and watched the two carefully. "What venture?" she said at last.

"He's going to buy Cleary's," Susan said, slurping her drink.

"Shut up, Susan," he said.

"Why not?" Jack said. "It sounds profitable."

Background music picked up. A lithe saxophone player in torn jeans warmed up on the small stage. Tables around them were jammed with young people dressed predominantly in black. Some wore olive shirts buttoned to their necks.

"No one knows about anything. It's a private negotiation. Cleary is overwhelmed. The place has pushed him over the edge. Monty Simms is the manager, but Cleary hates the way he's running it. He wants a new manager and someone to pass it on to. It was left to Leo by his great-grandfather. He was a piano player too, the original piano player — the 'Great One' they called him. But man, what an eccentric! They say he murdered someone right here in the club. As for Leo, his music and all take first place over the business and the mystery."

"Except for Miranda," Susan said, sarcastically. "And she'd die for the chance."

"Give it up, Susan," Tony said.

Even in the chaos of the club, several pairs of eyes turned on them. Glenda gulped her iced tea. Jack leaned over and whispered in her ear.

"Have I missed something? What's the problem?"

She watched Susan and Tony discreetly as they spoke tensely to each other.

"Not sure," Glenda whispered back. "Susan said something strange, though. Something about not 'wanting it to happen again.'"

"What not happening?"

"I don't know."

Even as she said this, her eyes went to the player piano in the corner, as if it involuntarily drew her attention. Why did she sense a connection between Susan's odd comment and the aged instrument? The lights went out to signal the start of the performance. Only candles lit the tables. As if under a spell, the crowd grew quiet.

In the mellow darkness, Susan spilled her drink and Glenda jumped back. The tablecloth appeared to bleed slowly as the red wine was gradually absorbed by the white cotton cloth. Tony glared at Susan over the flicker of the candle.

"*Susan*," he hissed, his tone a warning.

Then from the darkness came the sound of a smooth saxophone. A sliver of light illumined a young man in a black beret and red vest. But Glenda watched Susan's eyes, which looked glazed over somehow, frightened.

Soon the sax player drifted off to the piano and the stage lights came up. Then, blending one by one, rose the lazy, sexy sounds of clarinet, keyboard, light drums, guitar, sax, and piano, in succession.

Engrossed by the music, Glenda was surprised to see that Susan had disappeared, though Tony remained and watched the stage nervously. Jack leaned over to her.

"Look's like Susan's bored with jazz all of a sudden," he said in a low voice.

She shook her head. "Or afraid," she answered.

Jack gave her a look. Then the room went black. Glenda clutched Jack's sleeve. The jazz subsided, giving way to the sounds of a lone piano — the player piano. A spotlight came on, revealing a young man picking up the theme at the piano.

"Leo Cleary," Glenda whispered.

Jack nodded. "So that's the guy?"

From where she sat, Glenda could make out a mop of brown curly hair and dark beard. He sat relaxed, his movements fluid as his hands caressed the keyboard. The notes rolled from one octave to the next. His head swayed left and right as he played, his shoulders rising and falling, his body responding to the music, the piano seemingly alive with equal passion.

Glenda sipped her iced tea, watching the smoke from nearby cigarettes drifting in and out the shafts of light. She turned to see Susan staggering between tables, weaving her way back to their own.

At one point Susan paused, her gaze frozen on the figure of Leo Cleary at the piano. Oddly, she looked as if she might turn and run for the door. Instead, she pressed on to their table and sat down in some sort of trancelike state. All the while Leo Cleary played on, the notes sometimes quick and playful, then low and resonant.

Several hours passed. By one o'clock, most of the crowd had dispersed. A few hangers-on slurped drinks, their eyes droopy and red, fatigued with life and late-night bars. Glenda noticed that the occupants of the neighboring table, in black spandex and angular haircuts, now seemed locked into their own dimension. One striking woman wore a black sleeveless dress slit up the side. Strands of black hair tumbled around her pale shoulders, accentuating her melancholy expression. Legs crossed, her right leg bobbing to the music, she smoked a thin brown cigarette and eyed Leo intently. Glenda noticed that her black hose had a run starting at the ankle, where she wore black shoes tied with red ribbons like a dancer's slippers. Her comrades at the table rocked back and forth with laughter, cigarettes left unattended in the ashtrays.

Tony waved to Jack and pointed to the back of the club.

"Let me show you around," he said. "It's an excellent investment. Forget what some people say."

He glared at Susan as they rose. Jack took a last swig of beer as he too stood up. Glenda smiled at him. He rolled his eyes.

Some time after they'd departed, Glenda checked her watch, surprised to see that it was already two a.m. Leo Cleary played on, alone on the stage. The rest of the band had disappeared unobtrusively in the dim light.

Suddenly Glenda smelled something, something excessively sweet. Incense? Then smoke filled the room — an eerie lavender smoke. Glenda was alarmed to look around and see that only two other tables were still occupied. She looked to Susan, expecting her to appear unaware, sullen with alcohol, but instead found her eyes charged, her gaze locked on Glenda's.

"You feel it too, don't you?" she said, breathlessly.

Glenda didn't answer. Her feet felt strange. Was that sawdust on the hardwood floor? Why hadn't she noticed it before?

She looked at Leo Cleary now, his back to the crowd, and noticed a heavy burgundy curtain behind the piano. Beyond that was some sort of faded wall mural depicting an outdoor park scene like Grant Park or Central Park in New York. Why hadn't she noticed it before? And Leo's hair, which had been a curly mop half an hour before, was now slicked back with brilliantine.

Glenda sucked in her breath. Her mind tried frantically to solve this puzzle, to understand how the character at the piano had changed places with the real Leo Cleary. As she struggled to think clearly, the sounds from the piano changed. Then, dramatically, the tinkling, lazy sounds of modern jazz piano gave way to ragtime — a Scott Joplin rag from 1919.

The women at the next table rocked back and forth, oblivious to the change in tempo, all except the diva clad in black. She smiled from ear to ear, her eyes closed in some private ecstasy of sound and sensation, as if she were part of some sinister ritual. Glenda watched Leo beyond the young woman's head. He turned sideways on a swivel chair. His beard gone, he now wore a starched high-collared white shirt and dotted bow tie. What's going on? Glenda wondered, alarmed.

She sat up straight, feeling dizzy and light-headed. Faint and frightened, she tried to reach for Susan, but could not move. Suddenly the man at the piano turned and stared directly at their table, smiling broadly. His face was hard and surreal, like a puppet's.

Mouth agape, Glenda turned to Susan and saw that she had

slumped over in her chair. The trance had ended somehow. Glenda jumped to her feet and shook her friend by the shoulders.

"Few too many?" the woman in the slit dress remarked. "Disgusting how some people get, isn't it? Especially with all the help that's out there now." The other women at the table put their arms around each other's shoulders. One caressed the other's cheek.

Glenda grabbed Susan's wrist and felt for a pulse. The music had stopped; the ragtime pianist was gone. A single spotlight shone on the black piano top. Have I lost my mind? she wondered. The player section at the front had been opened to expose its inner mechanism. The blase group of women nearby conversed lazily, cigarettes going, feet up on the table.

Glenda ran into the spotlight and grabbed the microphone.

"Call 911!" she said, squinting into the dark room. "Call a doctor! Is there a doctor or nurse in here?" she said.

The room was dead quiet. Then a woman rose and moved toward the stage.

"I'm a doctor," she said. "What's the problem?"

"This way," Glenda said, directing her to the table. "It might be too late."

Lights flicked on. The doctor bent over Susan's inert body. Leaning closer, the doctor felt her wrist, then her neck. She stood up slowly.

"This woman is dead," she announced quietly.

A drunken woman in black spandex from the neighboring table screamed. Glenda searched the place wildly for Jack and Tony. Then her eyes shot over to the woman in black with the slit skirt. Unlike the rest of the group, the woman remained calm — eerily calm. Jack and Tony emerged from a stage door.

"Is she loaded again?" Tony demanded. "Jack, give me a hand here."

He started to grab her by the shoulders but Glenda pulled him back. "Tony, she's not drunk. She's *dead*."

Tony stepped backward, his eyes glazed. Jack felt Susan's wrist, then looked at Glenda in disbelief.

"What the hell happened?"

"I don't know, I just don't know," she stammered. "The room — it changed. The music changed! Susan and I were the only ones who noticed, as if the show were just for us."

"You and Susan?"

"Yes. She said she was frightened of being alone, in case it happened again."

"When did she say that?"

"Earlier tonight."

Chicago policemen rushed inside, accompanied by paramedics who surrounded the table, carrying a stretcher. They questioned Tony hurriedly, then marched over to Glenda.

The lights blinded her. Against the wall were straggling club patrons who had been detained, looking sullen, disheveled, and intoxicated.

"I told you," Glenda repeated to the police officer, "the place was pitch dark. Leo Cleary was alone on stage, finishing up his last set."

The officer frowned. "You been drinking too much, miss?" he asked.

"I don't drink."

He smirked.

"At all," she said, her mouth tight.

He nodded and made notes. "Who else was around besides you and the ladies at the next table?"

"No one as far as I could tell, unless..." she hesitated.

"Yes?"

"The only others would have been my husband Jack and Susan's boyfriend, Tony Manzetti."

Minutes later the club owner, Monty Simms, walked up. Glenda studied him intently as the police questioned him. His suit didn't quite fit, looking long in the sleeves and short in the pants. Oddly, the club itself had returned to its original modern decor, with a St. Pauli Girl beer poster on one wall and the musicians' folding chairs stacked neatly against the back of the stage. When had they cleaned up?

She jumped when Monty Simms tapped her shoulder. The police officer stood next to him and flipped through a note pad.

"What time approximately did you say you and the deceased gal, Susan Sedgeway, were watching this Leo Cleary guy finish up his set?"

Glenda looked at him, puzzled. Jack stepped up beside her.

"What's the problem?" he asked the officer.

"Well, Ms. Dominique here claims she and the Sedgeway broad watched Cleary finish up at around two a.m."

"Yes?" she said, looking from the officer to Simms.

"That's impossible," Simms said. "Cleary finished up at one. He'd already left. We pipe in music from the jukebox from one a.m. until closing every night."

"Ragtime music?" she said, hopefully.

Simms's brows furrowed. "Ragtime? What's that? We have funk, jazz, rock, you know, Talking Heads, Buddy Rich."

Jack put his arm around Glenda.

"That's impossible," she said, her voice tightening. "The women at the next table will confirm what I heard."

The police officer frowned.

"They're useless," he said, nodding toward the table. The women were slumped over, their heads resting on their folded arms. But the woman in the slit skirt had vanished.

"She's gone," Glenda murmured. "The other woman at the table. She was coherent."

The officer checked his notebook again.

"What other woman?" he said, looking up.

Chapter Two

Glenda sat back, fingers tapping the satiny arms of a French provincial chair. She raised her eyes to the high vaulted ceiling with its wooden beams and medieval chandelier. Then she looked over the other guests at the party. Jack had drunk too much already; she could tell by his overly animated conversation with a former professor from Northwestern University, his alma mater. Soon the professor moved on and Glenda grabbed Jack by the arm.

"I still don't see her," she said, clutching his sleeve. "Oh God, maybe I don't remember what she looks like! It's been a month since Susan's murder. No one will believe me now."

"No leads, no clues," he said, sloshing his drink as he rocked back and forth. "Chicago's finest can't figure it out."

"I've got to find that woman, the one whom no one else saw. Why did only I see her?"

Jack shook his head.

"There are enough characters here already."

"They're all music people — bohemians, eccentrics, hip professors."

"Thank God Dr. Glenn came with that music professor, the one all of you gossiped about like vipers. The one who sampled half the men in your freshman class — Carolyn Stind?"

"Right," she said, swirling the ice in her ginger ale.

A colorful group had gathered around a grand piano in the formal living room. Several boisterous young women belted out songs from *A Chorus Line*, particularly reveling in "Every Little Step She Takes." Glenda noticed one brunette in the middle, tall and statuesque, a purple nylon shawl with black beads draped over her tight-fitting yellow dress. With each arm, she embraced two other theater types.

Despite the suspicion surrounding his club and the demise of his

11

ex-girlfriend, Glenda thought Leo seemed to have jumped into this party with both feet. Strange enough to throw a party, Glenda thought, but to enjoy it so much too? He strutted around the room now, arms swinging by his sides.

"He's awfully nonchalant, don't you think?"

"I know," she said.

"His ex-girlfriend was just murdered a month ago. Tony didn't waste any time. I think Cleary dumped her only a year ago. I don't get it. Cleary's under suspicion, but he's acting untouchable."

"And surrounded by friends," she commented with a smirk as two women in purple sequins and red velvet bumped past her. "No matter how odd," she added. "They're his closest friends, but how close?"

"I'd worry with friends like those," Jack said, frowning.

The two women broke away and joined the gang at the piano. Leo sashayed through and the crowd parted. Jack laughed sarcastically.

"After what happened to his old squeeze while among 'friends,' I'd be careful if I were he."

Glenda nodded but said nothing, her eyes on the group around the piano. She noticed the striking brunette in purple lace, how she pressed her sleek body up against Leo's back as he settled at the piano. The brunette raised a wine glass to her glossy lips, then her eyes met Glenda's.

Half an hour later, the music had grown even more boisterous, and the woman in purple was guzzling her wine. Glenda noticed that the woman kept playing with her earrings. Set in an antique, blackish gold, the earrings had quarter-sized medallions or cameos, Glenda couldn't tell for sure. They looked familiar. And as the brunette grew more drunk, she fingered the earrings more frequently, stroking them like talismans.

Ten minutes later, the brunette wriggled through the crowd and swept out through the double glass doors behind the piano. Glenda watched the outline of the woman's body as she passed from the first set of doors to a second set at the right. A tiny spark flicked on in front of the woman's silhouette as she paused to light a cigarette.

Leo rocked from side to side at the piano, crooning a twenties-style blues tune while a woman dressed in red velvet harmonized in a low alto, her sultry voice filling the room, resonating in the high-ceilinged room like a sensuous embrace.

But Glenda couldn't forget the other woman, the one in purple, as she drifted back and forth outside, the spark of her cigarette still visible. The steps grew fainter as she took a last drag. Then she turned and entered the first set of doors. She stopped, staring, her alabaster hands still grasping the doorknobs. The party lights illumined her face. Even from across the room Glenda could see the intensity and rage in her eyes.

Leo didn't notice, so distracted was he by red velvet-clad arms and the laughing group. Glenda handed off her crystal goblet to Jack without looking up.

Suddenly the glass doors flew open and the woman in purple swept in. One by one, well-groomed heads turned. The women around him stopped singing. Leo did not relent. He continued to play until the woman stood directly in front of the piano, fingering her earrings nervously. Then his hands slowed and the notes died out. He looked up finally, following the others' stares.

The woman in purple scrutinized him, her mouth a straight line, her eyes glistening. Her face looked tired, creased, her eyes sad moons. She grabbed a fluted champagne glass from a waiter's tray, drank it in one gulp and replaced it.

"Good God, Claudia. What's the matter?" Leo asked. Claudia did not answer. Her gaze was steady as her tears flowed silently. No one moved. The tension was unbearable.

Leo simply started playing again, the ornamental women seeming to melt under his musical spell. Seconds passed like minutes. The woman in velvet leaned over and whispered in Leo's ear. He shook his head and kissed her cheek. Claudia turned and glided out the double doors again.

Glenda rose and walked over to a window and Jack turned back to the two professors. Thoughts sifted through her mind as she gazed out over the placid lake. She saw the silhouette of Claudia stalk across the wide lawn, a troubled soul growing increasingly unsteady in her gait until she disappeared into the darkness.

Glenda walked quickly to the next window, scanning the party briefly. The sound of tinkling glasses and fireside chatter seemed to fade, her mind working feverishly as she looked for Claudia.But the languid figure had truly vanished. Glenda felt uneasy, panicked. Claudia was gone.

Half an hour later, the party still raged on. Glenda settled back on a gold brocade couch in the corner, eyeing the French double doors. No one else, apparently, wondered about Claudia. People and drinks spun around Glenda. Nothing stopped. No one noticed.

Leo had wandered to a green divan next to the fire. The night continued to cool, growing too chilly even for a Chicago fall evening. Lake Michigan breathed moisture through the open French doors.

Something about the North Shore of Chicago had always drawn the wealthy to its privileged greenery, its fresh air, games of croquet and nights at Ravinia's outdoor music park.

This made Glenda wonder more about Leo Cleary. Why would a strictly city man, the renovated-loft type, live here on the North Shore? Flanked now by colorful women, he seemed to carry the jazz club with him, light and easy, somehow fitting gracefully into this suburban setting.

His calm, too placid demeanor seemed sinister. Glenda found his insensitivity about his recently murdered ex-girlfriend and his apparent disregard for Claudia's whereabouts both puzzling and maddening.

Glenda finished her seltzer water, set her glass on a marble side table, and paced, oblivious to the party. The eclectic nature of this artist's home, adorned with triangular abstracts right out of Soho, contrasted with the antique French provincial furniture, white velvet high-backed chairs and intricate polynesian and Oriental rugs. The contrast defied taste and somehow reflected a convoluted mind.

Pulling back the drapes on the floor-to-ceiling windows, Glenda looked out at the placid lake. She noticed, with some amusement, that Jack had rediscovered Professors Glenn and Stind. The two men smoked cigars, a sure sign that her husband was enjoying the party, while Professor Stind smoked a brown cigarette.

Swept up in her surroundings, Glenda had not noticed till now that a short blond man in dark glasses was watching her. His stare jarred her mind away from the festivities back to Claudia. Trying to appear casual, Glenda walked through the French doors to the veranda.

The air smelled fresh and the moisture off the lake formed dew on the windowpanes. The house, located at the top of a cliff overlooking Lake Michigan, was an example of North Shore architecture at its finest. Turning to look back at the house Glenda was reminded of a rambling Cape Cod, a back-lot set for Hepburn and Grant. The house spread from the left across at least an acre, its design following the line of the cliff sharply inward and outward. The horizon beyond the house hinted of midwest October, the clouds shifting past a full-faced waxing moon.

Until then, Glenda thought she'd seen the house. Yet now as she stood back she was amazed at the vastness of the place.

Someone touched her shoulder and she jumped. No one was there. She turned around several times, tugging her sweater more tightly around her, a lonely cold seeping into her bones. She rubbed her arms when a breeze picked up. Was that a moving figure far off, running along the lake? She couldn't be sure. The figure resembled Claudia.

Without hesitating, Glenda ran down the side of the hill until she reached a landscaped path. Claudia's dress looked torn, her steps along the rocks uncertain — or inebriated? Now and then Glenda lost sight of her in the trees. Was Claudia leading her somewhere, or running from her?

"Claudia! Stop!"

The woman didn't waver. All at once, purple fragments of her shawl fluttered and seemed to melt into the darkness. Rounding the corner, Glenda stopped, grasping a silky piece of fabric in her cold wet hand, looking left and right desperately.

She raced up the hill toward the house. Finding a side entrance, she stumbled into semi-darkness. Leo had the hallways lit in muted prisms of color with new-age music piped in. Several party guests lounged against the walls. Two men talked; another couple kissed in a corner. Glenda paused, not certain if she faced a real or imagined crisis. Had she become obsessed with the mysterious Claudia, as Jack had accused her of being? Should she make a scene?

One of the men in a ponytail looked at her distantly, as if in slow motion. A flashing light cast conflicting shadows around their profiles.

"Look, did either of you see a woman in purple run through here?"

The shorter of the two men stared at her. His eyes looked more alert than the other's.

"A woman? Not really. Do you mean a musician freak of Leo's? Or if she's one of these actresses he favors, they're all upstairs jamming around the piano. Right, Nick?"

The ponytailed taller man still looked at her vaguely, as if he couldn't make her out clearly.

"Right, man."

"Look," Glenda said. "This is urgent. She's not in her right mind."

"If she's loaded," the short one said, "she'll crash somewhere. Don't worry about it."

This was like a nightmare of running in place.

Groping her way along the darkened corridors, she found the back door again and stumbled outside into the purple night. The evening still felt cool, but now rang too dead, too still, unmoving. No cicadas of late summer belted out their alto trills. An obscure urgency seemed to be borne on the wind that whipped through the trees and in and out of her hair. She sidestepped down the hill again, her heart racing.

The music from the house reached her, competing with the loud pounding in her chest. She gazed at the lake. Did her eyes deceive her? A torn piece of purple fabric dangled from a branch of an oak tree overhanging the water. She ran down the hill and lunged for the swatch, but was stopped by the grip of an icy thin hand.

Chapter Three

A woman's voice shattered the silence. "Leo wants you inside."

Glenda turned when she felt the firm hand on her arm. The woman in red velvet, one of Leo's companions from around the piano, lingered in the shadows like something from a *film noir*. She looked pale, her complexion chalky, her crimson lips contrasting vividly with her skin. Had Glenda not felt movement in the woman's touch seconds before, she'd have thought her one of the living dead. The night itself felt lifeless suddenly, and somehow she felt it involved the woman called Claudia.

"How did Leo know I was out here?"

"He keeps track of all his girls."

"I'm no one's *girl*. I'm a friend of Susan's." She bowed her head. "*Was* a friend of Susan's."

The woman smiled a slow, eerie smile.

"She was one of his favorite girls. Look, he needs to talk to everyone to make an announcement. Where's the lovely Claudia?"

Glenda's eyes widened. "What do you know about her? What's her relationship with Leo?"

The woman in velvet smoothed her dress over her generous hips, her blue eyes looking bright, seemingly oblivious to Glenda's question. She took a deep breath.

"I'll tell him you'll be right in," she said, her voice deep.

With that, she turned on her high heels and stalked back to the house. A sudden darkness riveted Glenda to the spot; the spiderlike branches of the trees seemed to will her not to move. The woman in velvet diminished to a small speck on the hillside, soon illuminated by the back porch lights interspersed across the veranda.

As her form vanished in a flash of red through the French doors, Glenda heard the sound of an argument off to her right — first an angry male voice, then the terrified screams of a woman.

Edging her way down the embankment, Glenda crept closer. She could hear violent words and intermittent slaps, then the muted sounds of physical struggle. She'd have to act quickly. In the darkness, she could make out a blonde woman, wobbling on one spike heel, being shoved up against a tree by a dark figure. Sobbing, she had her hands to her face.

Glenda sprang forward to stop the violence. As she moved however, she tripped over a tree trunk of some sort. Then the soft, limp sensation made her realize it was no tree.

Recoiling in horror, she jumped back and sucked in her breath. There was not enough light from the moon and the back porch lights for her to see her own feet, much less the identity or condition of the corpse. The couple had disappeared. Had they already spotted the body, she wondered? Is that why they argued?

Chanting a childhood camp song like a mantra, Glenda turned and pounded her way back up the steep hillside toward the house, the tune rolling through her mind like a mnemonic sedative.

Finally she burst through the French doors and stood in the middle of the ornate living room, panting. Everyone turned to look at her.

"A body," she stammered. "I've found a body at the foot of the hill, next to the lake."

"What?" Tony demanded skeptically. "Who?"

Leo Cleary rose, the hands of his sultry admirers melting off his shoulders like wax. His eyes remained glued to Glenda's, his expression fixed as he walked to her.

"Sit down and tell me what you saw."

He pulled up a French provincial chair, looking too rugged for its fragile design. Despite her trembling, Glenda felt drawn by his soulful eyes and dark lashes. His dark, almost black hair fell across his forehead; his skin was fair, childlike in clarity yet somehow masculine, like some Renaissance prince. Perhaps this androgynous quality was what drew so many admirers, she thought suddenly.

He waited for her to speak, one firm hand on her shoulder. Glenda wiped away tears, looking up for the first time to see Jack standing at the back of the room with Professors Stind and Glenn.

"More lights," Cleary demanded, pointing to several men by the French double doors. "Flick the damn switch!"

All talking ceased. Someone brought her a glass of brandy but she moved it away. Jack worked his way through the crowd and handed her a glass of ice water. Not many people knew of her private battle with alcohol. She never touched the stuff, hadn't in ten years.

The woman dripping in gold sequins glared at Glenda. She took a position close behind Leo's back and massaged his neck.

"By the way Glenda, this is Miranda Gloucester, a friend of Susan's at one time. Now we're friends."

"Good friends," Miranda said, eyeing Glenda suspiciously.

Miranda's light brown hair, slicked back in a severe pony tail, left her face bare. Brown eye shadow and heavy liner on the top lids emphasized her large, doe-like eyes, eyes which would have worked far better on a sweeter face. Her chin and mouth looked homely until she smiled; then although sinister, she seemed sophisticated and beautiful.

"How could you have discovered a body?" she asked, accusingly, her voice low. "I saw you not ten minutes ago. You were alone."

Glenda sipped the water and set it down.

"I thought I was. Then I heard arguing. I wouldn't have intervened, except the guy was violent. I won't stand for that. I don't care how personal the situation is. I could see it was a blonde woman in a green striped dress. She'd lost one of her shoes. She had a dark tan and shoulder-length hair. And she was wearing a large, round hat. I know she wasn't at the party earlier."

Glenda did not mention that the blonde had been the witness from the Cleary Club she'd been searching for. She had no idea who to trust. Jack gave her a knowing nod.

"Who was with her?" Cleary asked.

"I only heard his voice," she said, her eyes distant. Then she hesitated. "He was angry at her," she continued, her voice trembling. "He pushed her up against a tree. I'm not sure if they'd already seen the body."

"I'll call the police," Jack said from the back of the group. "Where's a telephone?"

"Why don't we look at the body first?" Miranda said, turning a thick gold bangle around and around on her wrist.

Cleary rose suddenly. "Everyone stay put. Me, Griz and you," he said, pointing to Jack. "Let's go."

Glenda looked carefully at Miranda. She recognized her from having heard a lot of stories from her now deceased friend Susan. Susan had been at times inebriated, and at other times cogent enough to describe her nemesis more logically. Her friend had had numerous suspicions about Miranda but Glenda never knew when to believe her or when to assume it was drunken exaggeration. Either way, Glenda felt guilty now for not having taken Susan more seriously.

One of Susan's more wild tales told how Miranda had walked in out of nowhere one night, wearing leather and an attitude, and started singing at the club. At the time, Susan had been involved in a heated love affair with Leo Cleary and had not taken well to the new competition.

Eventually Susan's affair with Cleary ended. Around the same time, Miranda started singing at the club more regularly. Susan had suspected all along that Miranda was involved with Cleary. She referred to Leo as the "male whore of Lincoln Avenue." Susan also said, however, that she'd never had better sex before or since. Something about the "passion of a musician and the nimble fingers of a pianist." Now it didn't matter.

Jack walked over and knelt beside Glenda.

"You okay, kiddo?"

She took a deep breath and smiled.

"How will this look to the police? It's the second body I've found in a month. I'd suspect me if I were them."

Jack shook his head.

"Two other witnesses saw the body this time. You say the woman was blonde and tan?"

"Wearing a green striped dress. I know she was the witness I've been trying to locate all night — the one from the club, the woman in black. Why am I haunted by this woman? I can't even track her down!"

"What about the man? What did he look like?"

"It was too dark. The voice was familiar, though. An older man than us. Maybe in his mid-forties. God, if only I could place that voice!"

Then she spotted Cleary and two other men heading out the doors to the back hillside.

"Jack," she said quickly, hand on his sleeve. "Go with them. I have to have you to support my story or I'll go mad. Please go!"

"You sure you want me to leave you alone?" he said, looking around the room.

Miranda hovered near the punch bowl, talking with two other women, her eyes darting back and forth, but always returning to

Glenda. Most of the guests had cleared out long before discovery of the body. Now only ten or so hangers-on, the unfortunate suspects, remained in the room.

"I can't leave this room and I need to phone the police. I know what I saw."

"Thinking like a manager, honey — I already called the North Kenwood police. They'll be here shortly. Nothing ever happens on the North Shore."

She caught his arm suddenly, her eyes anxious. "Sometimes I think I'm going insane. What happened at the club the other

night? I know what I saw, Jack. The entire room changed; the music, the surroundings, and Cleary wasn't Cleary."

"Cleary wasn't Cleary?"

"I swear he was someone from another time, like the jazz age, you know? The nineteen twenties or thirties? I must be nuts."

Jack studied her carefully.

"Everything will be fine," he said. "Whether or not I understand you isn't important."

"Follow them, Jack," she said gratefully, nodding to the exiting group. Despite what Leo had said, Monty Simms and Tony Manzetti had joined him.

Jack jumped to his feet and joined the three men as they trudged over the stiff autumn grass, their heads disappearing over the hill as they headed toward the lake.

Just as Jack fell into step, Professor Glenn ran up and slapped him on the back. The moon now shone boldly, blue and cool over the somber party as they strode across the lawn.

"This is a crazy one, huh?" Professor Glenn said, sounding oddly jovial.

Jack nodded, half listening, half absorbed in the group in front of them. He'd heard about Professor Glenn's bizarre antics in and out of the classroom, such as frying insects in the lab and then sampling them like caviar just to prove a scientific point.

He'd heard a lot about Cleary too, from Susan, through Glenda. And Tony Manzetti, the other young man who walked in front of them — Susan's most recent lover — had known Cleary since college. The two had been music majors and roommates at the University of Illinois. Tony had always idolized Cleary, from what Susan had said. But Jack wondered now if Tony had known just how much Susan had cared for Cleary as well.

Walking with Professor Glenn, a short distance behind the group, Jack noticed that Tony rambled on to Leo, talking quietly as if to prevent Monty Simms from hearing. Leo turned and noticed Jack.

"Where did she say she saw him, Jack?" he said.

"Why 'him?'" Jack answered. "She didn't say it was a man."

"Him, her, whatever. Where'd she say? Closer to the lake or what?"

Simms stopped, looked around and lit a Salem menthol. Professor Glenn ran ahead and stopped suddenly. The menacing lake was now just ahead. Silence now left a vacuum in the night, filled only by the sounds of insects and a single distant car on the one-lane road beyond the house.

"Oh yes. Right here, guys. We have a dead one all right."

"Someone call the authorities."

"Already did," Jack said.

All eyes turned on him.

"That was pretty stupid," Manzetti said. "This could have been nothing and you'd have brought bad press on Cleary and the club."

"I know my wife. If she said she saw a body, she saw a body."

"This is interesting," mused Professor Glenn.

The well-dressed group of partygoers gathered around the large professor. Jack recalled that Glenda had told him the kids in college had always called him "Griz," as in 'grisly.' He'd never wondered about it until now.

"What do you make of it, Griz?" Jack said.

The professor turned, his face frozen.

"How the hell did you know my nickname?"

"A friend of yours from Indiana University. Besides, Leo called you 'Griz' just now. How'd you get it?"

He hesitated.

"I figured it was either the difficulty of my exams or because I had a penchant for grisly murders. We discussed them all — from the maniacally driven Lizzie Borden and her axe to the more macabre serial killers like Ted Bundy." His voice became ponderous, a monotone. "Kept the students awake in class — and probably up most nights."

"Back to the present, guys," Leo said. "Does anyone have a flashlight?"

"I have a pen light," Jack said, searching his dress pant pockets.

"There."

He tossed it to Leo, who flicked it on. The small beam of light flashed on a woman's legs, clad in fine lavender hosiery. She wore no shoes.

Jack felt a sinking sensation. He recognized the woman in purple from the party. She'd been alive just an hour before. And Glenda had mentioned that her behavior seemed odd. Why hadn't he listened to her?

"Oh my God," Leo muttered. "I just took a walk with her two hours ago."

"Here? By the river?" Jack said.

Leo nodded absently.

Griz crossed his massive arms over his chest. "Who is it?" he said.

"It's the babe who barged into the party," Manzetti said, cynically. "You know. The one by the piano who went overboard with the sauce. Reminded me of all the bitchy sorority girls who wouldn't date me in college at University of Illinois."

"The woman is dead, for God's sake," Jack said.

Griz knelt down and reached out to touch the body.

Jack grabbed his arm. "Don't touch anything until the police get here. They'll handle it."

"You really called?" Leo said, his voice sounding unusually reserved.

To Jack, Leo seemed inappropriately calm for someone whose former lover had been brutally murdered just a few weeks before. It bothered Jack now.

"Yes. Glenda said she saw a body, so I called the cops. What's the problem? There's nothing to hide here, is there?"

"That's another thing," Tony said, his voice derisive. "Why does your wife keep turning up bodies?"

Monty Simms lit another cigarette, one hand shoved in the pocket of his ill-fitting pants. The light from the small flashlight beamed across the cheap fabric of his suit, which Jack judged to have come from Mike's Suits on Diversey for about $299. He knew Susan had told Glenda that Simms was like a ticking bomb. The placid demeanor wouldn't last; something was on his mind. The other three men, Tony, Leo and Griz, also seemed to agree in some sort of silent conspiracy. No one spoke.

Forty minutes later, the crime scene roped off, a police officer and two detectives returned through the French doors. Jack spotted the familiar blue and gold of the North Kenwood police uniform. Now came the questioning. The officer's agonized face proved he'd seen more than drunken debutantes and illegally parked Jaguars tonight.

Jack scanned the room for Glenda. Miranda enveloped Leo in a steamy embrace as soon as he entered, leaning over him in the high-backed chair where he'd collapsed. He kissed her neck. She whispered in his ear intimately, her movements so sexual, that the overall impression became attractive in spite of her slouched shoulders and boyish chest.

Jack grinned as he approached Glenda. Then he stopped abruptly halfway. Griz was talking to her behind a row of built-in bookcases. Their conversation looked too familiar. Hadn't they met for the first time that night?

Chapter Four

J ack's mind worked frantically.

"Mister Dominique?"

He searched through his memories of the last four years. The move back to Rosedale, his new wife's home-town; his transfer to a new university and professorship; the encounters with her ex-lovers and her old demons. Yet now he recalled Glenda's ambiguous excuses on many late nights. Where had she been?

Someone put a firm hand on Jack's shoulder.

"What?"

The officer frowned.

"Why is it that everywhere we find a dead body lately, we keep finding your wife? I heard about the club scene downtown."

"What are you talking about?" Jack said, scanning the room.

"What the hell is going on? Why does she know everyone? First she's at the club on Lincoln Avenue, and now she's here on the uppity North Shore where there just happens to be another murder."

Glenda glided noiselessly across the room. Partygoers with hangovers lounged here and there, exhausted, as dawn approached. Several women slumped on a couch in the corner, smoking cigarettes, eyeing the policemen placidly. The woman in red velvet examined her legs, looking for runs in her stockings.

Glenda searched the room furtively, trying to gauge the mental condition of each individual. It had become apparent that all the suspects for tonight's murder were most likely all in the room.

Soon the homicide detectives took over as the police officer filled them in. Detective Halloran led the investigation. He and Glenda had been friends for years, since the days when Halloran had been an officer on the Rosedale police force. She'd actually assisted him on a previous case.

The younger detective, Detective Bykowski, betrayed his shock.

Murders just didn't happen in North Kenwood. Residents paid high taxes for snowplows in the winter, and top dollar for the best landscape gardeners in the summer. The town ordinances didn't allow residents even to park their yachts in their driveways, much less deposit messy corpses in their backyards.

"Is everyone here?" Detective Halloran asked, scanning the room. "We've searched the grounds. Is there anyone else in the house? And that includes any monkey business or sex going on."

"How big is this place?" Detective Bykowski said, chewing a large wad of pink gum. "Looks like a damn castle."

Detective Halloran waved away his questions and turned to Leo Cleary. "How large is this house, anyway?"

"I guess there are about twenty-five rooms, including the servants' quarters. It was built around the turn of the century, and has several levels. It's been compared to a rambling East Coast house like the one in the movie 'Philadelphia Story,' you know, with Katherine Hepburn?" he smiled, trying to appear charming. "It's been in the Cleary family for generations."

"Enough history," the officer said hastily. "We've searched everywhere. Are there any other rooms we should know about? Secret rooms?"

Cleary hesitated. "No."

Glenda circled the back of the couch where the two women stood and sat down next to Jack. She gave his hand a squeeze.

"Why are you questioning us like we're guilty?" Cleary said. "There's an entire room full of people here."

"And I notice it's the same people as last time," the officer said sarcastically. "What do you run, Cleary, a murder mystery weekend or something?"

Detective Halloran's eyes narrowed. "I heard about that strange murder at the club in the city. About a month ago now?"

Cleary sighed. "If you remember, I'd already left before the last murder was committed. I wasn't there. I was home. I had nothing to do with it. I can't account for all the unstable people who come to my club."

Miranda rose and grabbed her mink jacket. Simms moved toward the French doors. Detective Halloran raised his arms. "Enough! Everyone sit down. No one's leaving until the questioning is over. Officer Nelson, call for the crime scene team. Bykowski, you watch everyone here while Nelson and I scope out the situation more thoroughly."

Cold air burst into the room as the two left through the French doors, the same ones through which Claudia had swept out just hours before. Glenda watched the men disappear across the back patio and over the small hill, lit only by dangling Chinese lanterns strung up across the lawn.

Bykowski stood by the doors looking overwhelmed. Glenda studied the room again. Then her eyes went to Leo Cleary.

Monty Simms walked over quickly.

"Good old Miranda," he said to Glenda. "And that's Chick Natale in red. A wild one. Yet another singer."

"Friend of Leo's?" Glenda asked.

Monty nodded and walked off again.

Slouched between the two women on the couch, Miranda in gold sequins, and Chick Natale in red velvet, Leo Cleary looked lost, preoccupied. Miranda stroked his dark hair but he stared at nothing, his deep blue eyes intense.

Glenda drifted around the room while Jack conversed in a corner with Griz and Carolyn Stind.

Then the reality of her relationship with Griz crept into her consciousness. Had Jack seen them talking earlier? Would he even make any connection? After all, Glenda had been Griz's student and as far as Jack knew, that had been all.

Monty Simms paced, his shaggy blond hair hanging in his eyes, smoking one cigarette after another. Tony glared at Glenda, smirking, then walked over to her and put a hand on her shoulder.

"It's been quite a couple of weeks for you, hasn't it? We're all stuck in the proverbial mire. And old Leo there, the happening lady's man, is oblivious."

Glenda nodded, forcing cordiality. Her suspicions of Tony had started long before Susan had spouted off in a drunken stupor one evening about his sexual prowess. Susan had spoken of abuse too, both the verbal and physical, as well as possessiveness and intense jealousy. He'd always demanded to know where she was, even when she drove to the post office or went bowling with girlfriends.

Now he stood too closely to Glenda. His thick brown hair was pulled back in a ponytail. He wore a small gold hoop earring in his left ear and Birkenstock sandals on his feet.

"Why shorts?" she said at last, just to say something. "The dead of winter is around the corner."

"You and Griz get along, don't you?"

She felt goosebumps on her arms.

"What are you talking about?"

"You know," he said, leaning over to whisper in her ear. "A little extra credit going on in the undergrad days, huh?"

"You're full of it," she said, laughing it off. "And you seem to be getting over Susan's death pretty well, Tony. It's been what, four weeks?"

He leaned back with a frown and fingered his ponytail, eyeing the other guests. Bykowski circled the room, examining bookshelves and taking notes on a small flip pad.

"Does he know what he's doing? I have a feeling he got the badge to get the babes, you know?"

Sophomoric, yes. But Glenda found something about Tony attractive in a contemporary, careless way.

"You're still playing in a band, aren't you?" she said, changing the subject.

"I'm lead guitar and vocal in a small group called the Sexpots. We play Belmont and Lincoln Avenue now and then. Not as well known as old Leo, but we get around. I toured Europe last spring."

"Really?" she said, stifling a yawn.

"We started out in Salzburg, Austria. Lot of available girls there. But the music came first. Always has. The girls just happen. I've never had to work at that. It's amazing, beautiful really."

He laughed, with a broad grin that revealed fine white teeth. "I don't say that to be full of myself. It's just the way it is."

"I used to date shorter men," said Glenda, musing aloud.

"What are you, six foot one?" he said, trying to appear unruffled by her reference to his height.

"Five foot ten. And you're around five-six?"

He smiled again. "Five-eight, actually. I guess a lot of men would be shorter than you, huh?"

"Weren't you at college with Leo Cleary?"

"I knew who he was, but Susan knew him much better. I met him through her."

Bykowski stood before them, his blond curly hair mussed, his face chapped by the brutal cold. He looked preoccupied as he waited for them to finish talking, as if he needed more time.

"I need to ask you two to stay here until Detective Halloran has finished his questions."

"Fine," Glenda said. "I'm here with my husband, Jack. We'll help any way we can."

"You say you found the body, ma'am?"

"She's good at that lately," said Tony with a smirk.

Jack walked over and put his arms around her. She felt Tony's eyes on her. Pushing off the wall, he walked off casually toward the couch where Miranda and Chick sat. Chick smoothed the nap of her red velvet dress while Tony leaned over Miranda and planted a generous kiss on her mouth. Leo stood in another corner speaking with Monty Simms. Simms stopped pacing long enough to light another cigarette.

Glenda half listened to Detective Bykowski, painfully aware that Griz was staring at her. Her face burned.

Walks on college campuses came back to her; strolling past weeping willows after the first day of his Ear Training 101 class at the junior college nearby where she'd signed up for summer classes, or talks around DePaul's Lincoln Park campus, or Northwestern's in Evanston. She'd felt some strange but compelling attraction to him. Unlike theory class, where she needed to stay after class with the eccentric Professor Lionel — an oddball known for wearing black dress socks, khaki shorts, and chewing the side of his lip when he talked with morning donut still caught in his grey beard — she made up excuses to stay after with Prof Griz.

But after several classes and hours of performance lab, she'd run out of excuses for needing help in ear training. Finally she'd simply accepted one of his numerous offers of coffee in the cafeteria to discuss dominant seventh chords. Soon they'd moved on to Dempster Street and sifted in and out of coffee shops, always ending up at Schubert's on the corner.

Tall and burly as he was, many girls might not have shared Glenda's strong attraction to Griz. But his thinning blond hair and barrel chest somehow made him that much more unique. Of course, there'd been the usual overbearing men her own age to ignore at the time. She'd had her share of miserable dates that resembled wrestling matches at midnight in the fraternity houses. So Griz seemed to come out of nowhere like an overpowering intellectual lumberjack with his maturity, virility and experience. They'd shared cappuccinos at the Artist's Snackshop on Michigan Avenue after concerts at Orchestra Hall, or showings of new movies at the Fine Arts Theater. But then the brutality had started.

They'd left the Lake Theater in Evanston after a ten o'clock showing of *The Big Chill*. A frigid January night — much like tonight,

Glenda thought — they'd walked past an Irish linen shop. She'd paused to admire something in the window when a young couple passed by — a nondescript young man walking arm in arm with his girlfriend, an attractive brunette who resembled Glenda. They were no different than any other couple of Northwestern students, except that the young man had stopped to say hello. Glenda had dated him once the year before. Griz's entire demeanor changed on the spot.

From then on the evening had deteriorated. Glenda's simple responses to deceptively innocent questions from Griz escalated into a violent argument. His good Doctor Jekyll turned into Mr. Hyde, and Glenda saw a side of the man she'd never seen before. Soon after, he had shoved her up against her used red Volvo, several male students passing by had restrained him, and, much to her horror, several had recognized him.

She'd agreed to see him again after that night — perhaps under the spell of youthful ignorance. Still shaken by the death of her mother, she'd felt vulnerable, yet safe somehow even in the arms of a demon lover. Had she been given hindsight at the time, she'd have never seen him again after that first night.

Several months and two or three bruises later, Glenda had caught on. She also took in some meetings at a battered women's group off campus. No one could know. She wore her stupidity like a wreath of shame.

Jack squeezed her arm and she broke the gaze.

"What is it?"

She pointed to Detective Bykowski.

"You think that guy knows what he's doing?"

"Don't start."

"Someone has to look around who has some knowledge of how it's done. We need the city police here to do the job right."

"Go on then."

"I'll be discreet. I always am."

With that, she walked past the bookcases, past the couch where Miranda and Tony whispered intimately, and paused by the French doors where the group of investigators had passed. Soon the group ascended the hill and she saw them coming into sight. She stepped back to allow the entourage in.

"Okay," said Detective Halloran. "Everyone take a seat somewhere. You're all going to be here for a while."

Miranda sat up straight, frowning, her mouth set.

"What are you saying? We're *suspects*? Whose body did you find?"

"From what we can tell, it's a woman around the age of twenty-eight, wearing a yellow party dress and a purple shawl. She was clutching a piece of jewelry that looks like a dangling earring of some sort. She's been strangled."

Glenda scrutinized everyone in the room as the detective spoke. Miranda paled instantly. The woman in red velvet, Chick Natale, gasped out loud.

"My god! That's Claudia."

"And you are?" the detective said.

"Chick. I used to sing with her at a club off Diversey. We were roommates," she finished, suddenly bursting into tears.

"I knew that babe had drunk a little too much, or popped a few too many pills," Tony sneered.

"Shut up for once," said Miranda.

Glenda's stomach turned. She pulled away from the shadows and stepped into the middle of the group.

"There were other witnesses," she said firmly.

"Really?" asked Detective Halloran, his eyes intense. He pulled out a flip pad. "Describe them, why don't you? What did they look like?"

"I saw a blonde woman, wearing green. One of her shoes was missing."

The detective frowned. "Well, what did you hear? How did you know there was more than one witness?"

"Because I heard a vicious argument between a man and woman. I know the other person was a man, and I don't see the woman here," she said, scanning the room. "All I know about the man," she said finally, her eyes resting on Griz, "was that he was violent and angry."

"Now you're the one on drugs. Drinking too much again, Glenda? You never could control yourself." His eyes blazed.

"Nice try Griz," she said. "I haven't had a drink in ten years. Ten years and three months to be exact."

Griz's entire countenance changed as all the eyes in the room turned to him.

Chapter Five

The previous night's questioning consumed Glenda's thoughts as she strode briskly down Center Street in downtown North Kenwood. Despite the frigid morning air, her mind dwelt on Griz. She felt certain it was he who had argued with the missing witness, the blonde in the green dress. It made sense that a woman like that would be involved with Griz, she thought. All at once she halted in front of the North Kenwood Antiques Store. A large black-and white photo, framed in an authentic oval cherrywood frame, sat in the center of the display window.

"Oh my God!"

The photograph was encased in a rare oval frame, one of those so difficult to find since the turn of the century, in which the center of the glass arches in slight relief away from the picture. But this picture in particular made her stop. A very old photo dating from around 1920, it showed six members of a jazz band. Their faces looked waxen, spectral. None of the four faces in the middle looked familiar. One held a trombone, one a trumpet, one a saxophone, and the one on the far left sat behind a drum set. The face of the man on the right, however — the man with slicked-back hair seated at the piano — made Glenda's blood run cold. It was *him*. It was the piano player.

I'm losing my mind, she thought. She leaned forward, pressing her face against the glass. She saw the proprietor looking at her from inside. Within seconds, Glenda had entered the shop, pushing her way through the thick oak door, and approached the bemused woman whose glasses were perched at the tip of her nose. Another customer, a yuppie-looking young woman in her mid-thirties was examining the clocks along a far wall. Glenda stood on tiptoe and leaned over the railing of the window display, straining to see the photo more clearly. The proprietor shuffled past.

"Excuse me?" Glenda said, touching her arm.

"I'm with another customer," the older woman said. "I'll be with you in a moment. I can only handle one person at a time."

Glenda sighed at the owner's attitude — a haughty radar for the customer with the most cash. Yet if the woman only knew how long Glenda had been searching for confirmation of what she'd seen the night of Susan's murder! Now she'd pay any price.

The customer shook her head emphatically, tucking a lock of shoulder-length hair behind her ear, exposing a carat-sized diamond stud. Then she reached into her purse and pulled out her checkbook.

"I'll take the Austrian clock, the cuckoo. Is eight hundred okay for now? I'll come over Monday with the remaining three."

"Fine, Mrs. Langtry. Let me box that clock for you."

Glenda checked her watch. She had a therapy appointment in ten minutes. Were she late, she'd still have to pay the full ninety dollars. Then she got a break.

"No, no," the woman countered. "I'll pick it up on Monday. I have a manicure."

As the woman swept out the door, the proprietor jotted lengthy notes behind the cash register. After a moment she straightened up, as if noticing Glenda for the first time.

"Yes?"

"The photograph. The one in the window. I must buy it."

"Well now, isn't that interesting!"

"Why?"

"You're not the first person this morning to inquire about it. Someone else left a message on the answering machine — but he, or she, I couldn't tell which, got cut off. End of the tape," she said, apologetically. "Then I erased it by mistake. No one's come in yet, so I suppose you can have it."

Glenda felt light-headed.

"How long have you been open today?" she inquired quickly.

The old woman checked her Bulova watch, which bore the twisty "magic" band made popular in the 1970s.

"We've been open just twenty-five minutes. Mrs. Langtry knows our hours so I let her in early. I always treat the regulars with courtesy, especially in North Kenwood. People with money always know what they want."

"Right," Glenda said, panic taking away her breath. "I'm kind of in a hurry. If you could get the picture for me?"

The woman shuffled toward the display.

Now should that other person come in, I suppose, to be fair, I'd have to let you two barter. The price is three hundred and fifty as it is. It's mostly the frame. You can't find those oval arched frames anywhere, not any more."

"Three hundred and fifty dollars?"

The woman stopped.

"Is that a problem?" she said, peering at Glenda suspiciously over her spectacles.

"Not at all. Don't box it. Just brown paper or whatever."

Glenda stood back, arms crossed over her chest, watching the woman trying to reach for the photograph. She was clearly over seventy years old. Could she lift the heavy frame? Her practical wedge-heeled shoes lifted off the floor as she groped, reaching with difficulty for the photograph.

"Why don't you try the lock?" Glenda suggested.

The woman fiddled with the lock on the sliding door behind the display, then shook her head.

"I'm so scatterbrained on Saturday mornings! Wrong key! The right key is back in the drawer."

She trudged to the back of the shop and disappeared through a heavy curtain. Glenda calculated silently how to come up with the money after paying the month's bills. She and Jack had less than fifty dollars in their joint account. And to barter with someone would mean she couldn't take the photo away with her. Who else would be interested enough to have already left a message on the answering machine, she wondered?

"How long has the photo been in the window?" asked Glenda when the old woman reappeared. She stopped in her tracks to think and Glenda regretted her question.

"That photograph? I think it's been there since last Wednesday."

"That's all?"

The older woman nodded absently as she held up a ring of tinkling keys, then paused. "It *is* kind of strange how fast someone responded."

As she listened, Glenda looked out into the street. The quaint downtown square with its old brick buildings seemed unfriendly and sinister somehow. Then Glenda saw something on a nearby corner that made her jaw drop. On the corner stood Miranda, her hair pulled back in the same severe style she'd worn at the party. She was apparently waiting for the light to change, for as soon as it did, she hurried toward the antique store.

Was this the mysterious caller? wondered Glenda. She turned to the old proprietor, impatient with the woman's ponderous movements. "Let me help you," she said, springing forward.

"I've got it," the proprietor said triumphantly, grunting as she heaved the photo out from its space.

As she waited, Glenda noticed another familiar face — Monty Simms, nervously smoking a cigarette as he rushed to meet Miranda. They embraced briefly, then began an animated conversation directly in front of the antique store.

Glenda stood in the back, hidden by dusty bookshelves, pretending to read a book by Jonathan Swift. She looked up periodically, keeping tabs on the pair outside. Their conversation grew heated. This ran counter to a fundamental unspoken rule: North Kenwood did not allow public displays of any kind — not intimacy, not affection, and especially not anger. Domestic bliss or misery were usually restricted to the confines of one's own property. Even the proprietor of the antique shop paused to stare when Miranda slapped Simms.

"Young people nowadays," the woman commented, shaking her head. "Never know what will set them off."

Glenda nodded when the woman looked to her for confirmation. Taking a deep breath, Glenda looked up at the high ceiling where a fan turned slowly. Behind her, a second-level balcony overlooked the room. Every available wall housed books, floor to ceiling, except at the back where an oversized mirror hung behind the cash register. Glenda followed the proprietor to the register and continued to monitor the two on the sidewalk in its reflection.

Miranda, in a black turtleneck, voluminous black overcoat, and black leather gloves, looked like something out of a German film. Glenda thought she'd overdone it in Chanel — her purse, even the heels of her shoes bore the Chanel logo. Her usual severe ponytail exposed antique-looking earrings, except this time she'd braided her hair and fastened some sort of beaded gold barrette on the end.

Absorbed with the two arguing on the street, Glenda failed to notice a lanky young man with dark hair jaywalking his way across Central Street. In his hurry, he nearly collided with an older woman on an English lightweight bicycle, dashed around a woman with a stroller, and headed straight for the antique store.

Seconds later a car screeched to a halt, just missing a young couple. Everyone turned to look except the young man, several strands of blackish hair dropping in his eyes. He pressed his face to the glass. Glenda intuited something. Even a first edition of Hemingway wouldn't cause such a clamor. She turned back to the proprietor, who was now struggling to get the string around the brown paper on the package. A grey-haired gentleman in his mid-fifties came to the cash register from behind a curtain in the back of the store.

"Can I help, Jeanine?" he said.

She made a face. "Thanks, Herbert. I'm having quite a time with this frame and I still need to pick up our breakfast pastries — the North Kenwood Garden Club is coming over this morning. Would you finish up this job for me? The young woman's all paid up."

Glenda whipped around at the tinkle of the brass bell over the front door. In the mirror's reflection, she saw the young man enter the store. Jeanine disappeared through the curtain. Herbert started on the string.

At the same time, Miranda turned toward the display window, gesturing dramatically, only to look shocked at the sight of empty space where the photo had been. Glenda had to get out of the store right away. The photograph was her only proof that she did see something strange that night at the club.

"This is troublesome, isn't it?" he said.

The young man searched the display window. Something made Glenda step up. Herbert smiled, remembering Glenda from her childhood, when she and her mother made trips from Rosedale to North Kenwood just to find old Nancy Drew mysteries and jewelry boxes.

"You know what, Herbert? I'll just take it as is."

"Fine, Glenda. What is it, anyway?"

The young man stalked over to the counter.

"Where is it?" he demanded.

Herbert looked up over the tops of his bifocals.

"Excuse me, young man. I'll be with you in a moment."

"Thanks, Herbert," Glenda said hurriedly, shoving the package under her arm. "See you soon."

She nodded at the young man as she ran past.

Herbert looked startled. "Okay, bye Glenda," he said, waving, having already forgotten what he'd asked her. "See you." He turned to the young man. "What can I do for you?"

"The photograph. Where the hell is it? I called about it last night."

Herbert frowned. "Slow down, sir, and describe it. I don't know all the inventory by heart. Where'd you see it?"

"In the *window*," he said, waving wildly at the display window. Glenda paused by the front of the store, her hand on the doorknob. "Don't tell me you've sold it out from under me!" he persisted. "Is this the way you people do business on the North Shore? I have to have that photograph!"

Herbert emerged from behind the counter, his knees creaking and slightly bent as he walked stiffly toward the display. Glenda slipped out and hurried down the street, clutching the photograph under her arm like a running back heading for the end zone.

She ran for several blocks until she reached the elevated train, panting. Hopping onto an Evanston express train, she hugged the frame to her chest. She had determined to compare the photo with the club itself. Once on safe ground, she would confirm what she thought she'd seen in the photo the first time.

Minutes later, Glenda got off the train and walked from the corner of Lincoln and Fullerton Avenues toward the club. Before she could, she ducked inside a diner on the corner when she spotted Griz leaving a costume shop across the street. A busy intersection, she had trouble deciphering through cars whizzing past, just what kind of costume he carried. All she could make out was a black zippered bag slung over his shoulder.

Finally, she emerged from the diner. She had to get inside Cleary's to compare, to remember for certain that macabre night when the specter had appeared to her alone in some sort of singular side show.

Glenda tried the front and side doors; both were locked, so she walked around to the back. Spotting a cement kiosk, she decided to sit down and take a quick look at the photograph.

After making sure she was unobserved, she removed the brown paper, stared at the photo and stiffened. It couldn't be, she thought. She leapt to her feet and put her ear to the back door of the building. It was unmistakable: she could hear the faint tinkling of an upright piano from inside the bar. Instantly she recognized Scott Joplin's "Maple Leaf Rag," the same forceful, upbeat chords that had filled the club from the floorboards to the rafters on the night of Susan's murder. Now, however, the music sounded eerily jubilant, as if victorious.

Once more Glenda sat frozen, listening to the sinister music. The photograph still lay on her lap. Once again, she was the only witness to a menacing performance. But the musician who played now seemed unafraid of detection, playing with abandon, pounding each chord joyously. She could feel his arrogance and cunning in the very confidence with which he played, the upper register clear and graceful as it built in crescendo. Oddly, Susan's description of musicians as lovers came to her; "passion and skill all in one." And as murderers?

Dazed and outraged, she set the photo on the kiosk and backed away from the club, the music drawing her in to its rapture nevertheless. Bewitched by the intoxicating jazz rhythm, Glenda never heard the screech of brakes or the wail of a car horn. In her mind, the jazz era reigned once more, and soon the torment of murder would resurface.

Chapter Six

Glenda squinted, a bitter taste in her mouth, the nausea overwhelming. Blinded by white and grey clouds shifting aimlessly overhead, she wondered why she didn't fear being run over. After all, she'd just been hit by a car seconds before. Then voices reverberated and car doors slammed. A female voice yelled for someone to call an ambulance, and then the lightheaded serenity of the treetops against the puffy white clouds was shadowed as someone leaned over her.

"Don't move," said the female voice. "How do you feel? We've called an ambulance."

A stocky taxi driver stood in the street pointing maniacally at Glenda, then walking in circles, apparently re-enacting the crash. His movements were exaggerated, his speech broken. Glenda sat up and took a deep breath.

"I think I'm fine," she said. "He wasn't going that fast."

She began to stand up and the woman, whom she now saw to be a police officer, pressed her firmly on the shoulder.

"Take it easy. We have to let someone have a look at you. Help will be here any minute, okay? Come on, do me a favor and don't move. What was your hurry anyway?"

Glenda rubbed her forehead with her hand, running her fingers through her sandy bangs, trying to concentrate. Then she remembered.

"The photograph!" she said, straining to see the kiosk around the crowd that had formed. "And the music, that strange music..." She grabbed the woman's sleeve. "Someone has to believe me now!"

As she turned back to the kiosk where she'd left the photograph, she saw a young man in a purple Northwestern University sweatshirt, and recognized him from the antique store. He grabbed the photo and took off running.

"Stop!" Glenda said, rising and stumbling after him. Soon he dropped out of sight around the corner of Diversey and ran away down Lincoln Avenue. Glenda kept pace with him for a block, then slowed down under a passing elevated train, leaning over, dizzy, hands to her knees as she tried to catch her breath. The police officer caught up to her and when Glenda straightened up, she saw the young man hop on the el train, the brown-paper-wrapped photograph clutched under his arm.

"I don't believe it," she said under her breath.

"What the hell are you doing, lady? You've just been hit by a car!" the officer admonished her.

Glenda stepped back, shaking her head, hands on her hips. "I've just been robbed."

"We can fill out a report after you're checked out at St. Joseph's Hospital," the police officer said, guiding her to the squad car parked near Cleary's Club. "Was it something expensive?"

Glenda sighed and kicked the sidewalk with her toe. "Priceless."

The next morning was Sunday. Jack rubbed Glenda's neck while she recounted the previous day's events. One bulb had burned out of their dining room chandelier, making the room, on this typically dark fall morning, even dimmer. Dust and shadows darkened the wooden floors, and the aged wallpaper, and cherrywood trim. Glenda stiffened, recalling the loss of the old framed photograph.

"What's the problem?" he said. "You have to relax."

"I can't. That picture was my only shred of proof. No one will believe me without it."

"What did it show, anyway?" he said, stopping and sitting across from her at their simple prairie style table.

"It was a picture of five or six members of a jazz band from around —" she began, stopping, checking his face, "from around nineteen twenty." She grabbed a pencil before he could answer, ripped a piece of paper from a nearby electric bill, and began to sketch. "Look, it was five or six musicians; I can't be sure. And then in the back, right here," she said, drawing a curtain, "there was this weird tapestry or something. The thing is, the only other time I'd seen it was that night at the club, the night Susan died and things — *happened*. The photo was taken at Cleary's."

Jack looked at her, his face solemn.

"What good was it to you?"

I saw Cleary in the picture. Leo Cleary."

Jack rolled his eyes. "It could have been his great grandfather, or some relation."

"Don't you see? It was proof that what I saw was there decades before. Something metaphysical happened that night."

"Here we go again with the supernatural ghost talk. Someone could easily say you'd seen the picture somewhere before, that it was suggested to you."

"Was Susan's murder a suggestion?" Glenda rose and began to pace up and down.

"What does Susan's death have to do with what you say happened that night?" He turned to watch her as she moved restlessly around the room.

"There was something crucial in that photograph. It had details I need to inspect — clues to Susan's murder and the bizarre events at the club. I know this sounds crazy, but I recognized a woman in the photo."

"There was a woman in the band?"

"Yes. And I'd swear she wore the same earrings that Claudia person was wearing when she was murdered. Women notice earrings and jewelry, Jack. Remember, the police found her clutching only one earring. So where's the other one?"

"What was the name of the band in the picture?"

"That's what I don't know. But whoever they were, the place was definitely Cleary's Jazz Club. It looked to be around 1915, 1920."

Jack hit the table with his palm.

"That's right!" he said. "How could I have forgotten to tell you?"

"What?"

"At the party the other night I got to talking with those two professors, you know, Stind and Glenn."

"I noticed," replied Glenda with a wry smile. "A little more with Stind, I think. She has a reputation for liking young men, you know."

"I guess I'm safe then," he said, smiling. "No, really. I think Griz — you know, Professor Glenn — mentioned something about the history of the Cleary family and the jazz club. Some sort of scandal, from the turn of the century or not long after, that involved Leo's great-grandfather. He was mixed up with some married woman, someone named Rose Green. But listen to this: the woman ended up murdered, as did her lover, a Doc Reilly, suspect."

"My God. You're kidding!"

"Griz also said that Cleary's was purchased, set up and run in the beginning by some rich undergraduate fraternity brothers from Northwestern University, right here in Evanston."

Glenda stopped pacing and looked at him.

"What is it?" he said.

"The young guy who swiped the photograph was wearing a Northwestern sweatshirt. It might be nothing, but there might be a connection."

"Too coincidental."

"Was it a coincidence that he showed up first at the antique store and then at Cleary's? He obviously followed me."

"You're sounding paranoid," he said.

"You still have your graduate school library card?"

"For Northwestern?"

"Yes. I'm going to the music library. There must be something in the archives about early bands and those fraternity brothers, maybe something will shed some light on Susan's murder. And what about Claudia and Leo? What was their relationship?"

"Seems like old Leo has a relationship with every woman he comes in contact with," Jack commented.

"What do you mean?"

"Well, at the party for instance. How many women there do you think he's slept with? They all knew him pretty well."

"There *is* something about him, I must admit," agreed Glenda dreamily, "even his house. And his taste was so eclectic and flamboyant. It didn't seem like it was all *him*, you know? I couldn't quite figure it out. It was as if someone else had a hand in it, like he didn't really live alone."

Jack looked befuddled.

"What is it?" she asked.

"I have a bad feeling, that's all."

"I thought premonitions only happened to us intuitive womenfolk?" she said, laughing.

He looked serious. "I'm worried about you. I mean, what if that taxi hitting you was no accident?"

"Come on. The guy could barely speak English! I heard him trying to explain to the cops what happened. If he was a plant, then he deserves an Academy Award. Look," she said, hand on his shoulder, "I've got to get going. Give me your library card so I can get into Northwestern's music library."

"You might not need it there."

"Give it to me anyway, doll. It can't hurt."

"Ran into that Tony Manzetti character yesterday," he said, reaching into his jeans for his wallet.

She stiffened, then frowned.

"Where'd you see him? He's a creep. There's something about him I don't like."

"Could it be," he paused, "that he's a sexist womanizer?"

"Come on, Jack. The library card, please?"

"Well, you know I'm helping Cleary with some sound problems he's been having at the club."

"What do you mean?"

"At the party, he asked me to come over to his house yesterday morning and look at some electronic equipment. Manzetti was at the house."

"They were friends?"

"They were roommates in music school at the University of Illinois back in the late seventies. I don't know if former bunkmates constitutes friendship, but let's say they know each other. Manzetti's really into the music scene — has no talent himself but he tries to help Cleary in the business."

"That's odd. They're so different."

Jack gave her a careful look, reaching into a fruit bowl on the table and taking a bite from an apple.

"How do you mean, oh analytical one?" he said.

She looked agitated.

"You know," she said, cautiously. "Leo is so naturally creative, almost in an intuitive sense."

"Oh Leo, Leo," he cooed in a falsetto voice.

"No, I mean they're just totally different people. I don't understand how they could even be friends."

"Former roommates."

"Still in contact."

She paced around the dining room, her favorite thinking room.

"I'm going," she said, taking the library card from him.

*****

Forty minutes later, Glenda was driving through the elegant and wealthy streets of Evanston, circling around the final curving mile of

Sheridan road to Northwestern's music library. Passing fraternity row, the regal red-brick Tudor houses with their rambling green ivy created a misleadingly peaceful scene. She recalled herself shamelessly drunk at parties in some of those houses, when as an undergraduate at DePaul University she'd crashed those same hallowed walls where normally only fellow classmates were allowed to tread.

At a stoplight outside the engineering building she glanced up at the sky over the lake, and the angry-looking clouds reminded her of her childhood days in Illinois. She recalled trying to cross a busy street in Rosedale where she'd grown up, an impending tornado whirling around her as she stood shivering on the corner in her one-piece bathing suit, with only a beach towel to protect her from flying gravel and dust. That same turmoil permeated her senses at this moment.

Now as she sat at the stoplight she felt the anxiety of a storm about to hit. The pregnant swell in the atmosphere filled her up; the moist air seemed both to revive her spirits and fill her with dread. She rolled down the driver's side window and then the passenger window to watch a group of college men playing soccer on a field near a fraternity house. Their frenetic energy calmed her jangled nerves.

She took a deep breath, then pulled away from the stoplight.

In the next block she turned right, parked in a lot, and walked across the green expanse of grass outside the music library. The sky rolled into a grey curve overhead and she ran the rest of the way. Suddenly, she felt she had been dropped into a strange land, some suburb she'd never seen, and the pressure in the air sucked the life out of her. She felt the pressure of Griz in her memory and for some reason she panicked as she reached for the doorknob to the library.

In the foyer of the building she paused. The vast hallway smelled archaic, the tiles on the floor uneven under her feet. She climbed the stairs, gasping as her hand touched an odd winged gargoyle; its cold cement surface felt clammy.

She read the hours on the door plaque of the library and walked in to find a librarian hunched behind a small oak desk.

"Excuse me?" Glenda asked, trying to whisper.

"Yes?"

The woman's voice was both hushed and appropriately musical. "I need to see the historical archives about the music department here. Would that be possible?

"Library card, please."

Glenda fumbled in her purse and handed it to her. A Cheshire-cat smile spread across the woman's face.

"This way," she said, arthritic hands pushing off the desk as she rose laboriously.

As Glenda followed the librarian, a flash of green outside the window caught her eye. It was a young woman with a striking tan wearing an ill-fitting leather jacket over a green dress. At first Glenda just laughed to herself — she and Jack often spoke of handing out what they called "fashion citations" to people wearing such abominable combinations. Then Glenda's heart skipped a beat. Although the woman was wearing a scarf, Glenda could see her pale blonde hair and remembered her green dress from Leo's party. Her hosiery had numerous runs and she wore only one shoe. As the woman passed by the window across the lawn, Glenda could see bruises on her face. Where had she been for the last two days, Glenda wondered, alarmed.

Before she could move, an old 1968 Mercedes Benz pulled up. Someone yanked the woman in green into the car and sped away down Sheridan Road.

Chapter Seven

Glenda ran to the window of the library, squinting desperately to make out the license plate of the rusted-out silver Mercedes as it sped away with a woman whom no one else, save Glenda believed existed. At the same time, a brooding storm had left much of the sky in the East awash in a smear of charcoal gray, an angry darkness hovering over Lake Michigan and the campus of Northwestern like a fuming god. Glenda had forgotten her mission until the old librarian seized her arm in a claw-like grasp. In the dim light, the small woman's bright eyes shone like two anxious sparks. Although she appeared frail, with slight shoulders and grey hair pulled in a tight braid, her grip felt strong.

"Here are some of the archives I think you'll want to see," she said, indicating a glass case. "Most of these documents are original music compositions. The only photographs we have are here," she said, walking to a locked bureau. She tugged at the drawer and when Glenda stepped forward to help, the lights dimmed.

"Damn these storms," snapped the librarian. "In this old building, the lights always go first." She stopped. Glenda knew the librarian was watching her. "Since we're friends in this calamity, call me Helen. And now this drawer."

She yanked on it again. Glenda envisioned the old woman toppling backwards, the bureau crushing the life out of her.

"Let me help, Helen."

"No, no. I'll get a flashlight. There must be one in the desk drawer."

Glenda heard shuffling sounds as the woman's soles crossed the wooden floor. Her return was illuminated by the narrow beam of a tiny flashlight. Outside, the storm winds lifted leaves and debris into eddies — tiny cyclones on the sidewalk foretelling a tornado. Yet something stirred within the room as well, a heady whirl that seemed to emanate from the mosaic ceiling, though Glenda saw no ceiling fans. And the floor under her feet felt not quite solid; in fact, her heart jumped and she felt gravel or wood chips — no sawdust — scraping under her heels.

Another window had been opened wide to admit the Indian summer breeze, yet now the temperature had dropped twenty degrees. In momentary flashes of daylight, Glenda saw objects from the old woman's desk scatter to the floor. Papers, stamp pads, overdue-book slips, and paper clips covered every inch of space. She recognized the mottled black-and-white tortoise-shell design of a 1928 Parker Duofold fountain pen on top of one pile of debris.

Crouched over the bureau, Helen shone the flashlight into the file cabinet, flooding the insides of the drawer. The two women peered into it like curious sprites opening Pandora's box. Tabs divided the files by dates; various tabs were darker than others, some more faded than others. The scent of aged paper, like the middle of a first-edition volume, drifted upward. Glenda searched for the files for 1900, 1901, and 1905. Several years appeared to be missing.

"What exactly are you looking for?" Helen asked, looking up, the light shrouding around her face like some eerie halo.

"I'm not sure, really. May I just look through here?"

"No."

The lights flickered and stayed off in a dead, final way.

"No?" repeated Glenda, incredulous.

"They're rare photographs. I can't let just any student who drops a nickel in the nickelodeon handle them."

Glenda looked at the woman quizzically. "Well, I'm not a student," she said, letting the reference to a decades-old song pass without comment. "I'm investigating a murder."

She heard the librarian inhale sharply.

"Are you with the police?" Helen whispered.

"No, but a friend of mine was murdered and I have to get to the bottom of it." After a thought she added, "The situation was highly suspect." She hesitated. "Don't think me insane, but I believe that *netherworld* forces were involved."

The air from outside filtered in quickly now, in wavelike gusts, as if they stood on the shore of Lake Michigan. From the sounds of it, Helen had turned away from Glenda, muttering.

"*Praise ye the Lord,*" she said almost inaudibly. "*Sing unto the Lord a new song and his praise in the congregation of saints.*"

Thunder boomed, and Glenda felt the vibration in the floor under her feet.

"Excuse me?"

"*Look to the ant, thou sluggard...*"

"Ma'am?"

A shattering crash exploded outside followed by a low bass rumble which rolled through the room.

"*In the name of the Father, the Son, and the Holy Spirit, Amen.*"

"Are you all right?" Glenda said at last.

"Ghosts, you say?"

In the shadows, punctuated by a momentary flash of lightning, the woman's eyes looked ironic, knowing and grey.

"I suppose if you could specify a year, I could give you that file. Illinois has had its share of spirits. The city of Chicago has more legends than any old West ghost town. Here's the flashlight."

"Thank you, Helen. Please give me the file for 1908. I'll start there."

Another gust of wind blew in the open windows and Glenda shivered. The air was reminiscent of summer nights in Grant Park for Tchaikovsky's 1812 Overture, when the lake would turn the air as suddenly cold as a temperamental lover, and listeners would pour more wine and snuggle up in their Canadian trapper blankets. She unrolled her sweatshirt sleeves and scanned the files by the beam of the flashlight, black and white glossies in their protective sheets flipping past. The faces in the photos looked ghastly in the meager light.

The sky outside the window had turned sickly yellow, a further indication that the tornado was about to hit. On the bookshelves, even the spines of the books themselves seemed to lack color; only shadows prevailed. Dimension in the room was measurable only by lighter or darker hues.

Helen pulled out the file for 1908. Each photo contained a label on the top right identifying the locale. The first, *SAE Fraternity*, was followed by *The Old Stadium, Music Library* (formerly *The Church*) and *Songbirds*.

"Stop. May I see the last one?"

"The old church?"

"No. The Songbirds."

Helen's eyes narrowed and as the beam of light flew past her back to the drawer, Glenda recalled how her sister, as a child, used to hold a flashlight under her mouth to frighten Glenda at Halloween.

"Of course that's what you want to see."

As Helen handed Glenda the file, the lights clicked back on to almost full capacity, yet still dusky. They moved to a long oak table nearby where Helen set the file down.

"Can you see?" she asked.

Glenda nodded, her attention focused on the file. Helen walked away silently, loftily. A queenly elegance quite unlike her plodding nature of ten minutes before.

As the file was opened, a rush of something imminent, something frightening, overwhelmed her. Immediately she recognized a familiar face: Leo's murdered great grandfather. According to Susan, she remembered, Johnny Cleary had been the musician to watch in 1919. The photo didn't tell her much now. It showed him in a Songbird Club photo. Perhaps that had been the name of the group which had launched Cleary's?

Glenda played devil's advocate with herself. Okay, she surmised, if the specter of Johnny Cleary was now haunting his own club, why had he picked *her* out from the crowd to be a witness?

And why, how, had Susan died? As Glenda thought about her old sorority friend from the University of Illinois, she still couldn't believe Susan was really dead. Granted, there'd always been a drinking problem, but Susan had always been bigger than life; she'd been youth epitomized. And although the coroner's report was still pending, the initial report said only that "the deceased may have been poisoned." But how? Glenda hadn't observed anyone near her friend. The only one who'd been near the drinks had been Tony Manzetti. Susan's lover. Suspicions usually did point to lovers and spouses, after all. Glenda knew her friend Detective Halloran from the North Kenwood police would fill her in on the conclusions of the autopsy. It seemed obvious that the apparition at the piano had occurred at the moment of Susan's murder for a reason. What was it?

Then Glenda thought about Claudia, the odd, suffering woman in purple wandering through the party two nights before. Why had Leo Cleary been walking with her by the water? Why a party at all so soon after a friend's death at his club? And those earrings...long, drop earrings that were distinctly antique. They'd looked from a distance like ornate cameos. Claudia had been fingering them meditatively at the party just before she'd disappeared out the French doors for the last time.

And why had Susan been murdered in the first place? Who would have wanted Glenda's friend dead? What kind of trouble was she in? Susan had always yearned to be the center of attention ever since Glenda had met her as a freshman in college. But Miranda Gloucester, a woman Susan had disliked intensely, had seemed overly interested in Leo Cleary at the party, even after the discovery of Claudia's body. The ensuing investigation by the police, even during the taking of photographs and the grueling hours of questioning of guests at the party, had not seemed to faze Miranda.

Glenda recalled now, looking up for a moment as the cool air flowed in through the window facing the lake, the look in Miranda's eyes as the investigators questioned her. It had been cool, almost icy. Much of the time she had seemed intent upon Leo, as if hypnotizing him or forcing her will on him. Her cat-like blue eyes had seemed to follow him even as the North Kenwood detectives questioned her.

Looking at another photo in the file, one of the young men in a group photo, actually reminded Glenda of Monty Simms, the present owner of Cleary's Club. He was another character, Glenda thought. So nervous all the time. During questioning by the police at the party, he'd paced back and forth, chain-smoking Marlboros from a crumpled pack. A switch of brands. How strange, she thought.

Glenda flipped to the next cracked and faded photo in the historical file, hoping to find the same telling picture that had been stolen from her by the young man in the Northwestern sweatshirt. One photo showed a group of young women seated for a club picture. Nothing outstanding struck her about it at first until she realized the jazz club was Cleary's.

Suddenly Glenda sat up straight, goosebumps on her arms.

Thunder crashed outside and rain fell in a torrential downpour. The night of the party came alive in her memory as she gazed outside, lost in concentration.

Miranda Gloucester. Glenda shivered. Why had Susan feared and despised the young woman? Glenda pulled a sweater out of the duffel bag she'd brought along. Now Susan was dead. As Glenda buttoned her sweater, she looked around the cherry wood walls of the library thinking it odd that no one else chose to study on a rainy Sunday morning. The moist smell in the room brought out the aged wood, the dust, the decades of reflection and learning that had taken place within these grey stone walls. A panicky sense of being alone overtook her.

The walls seemed to creak with the pressure of the storm outside.

This building has stood for at least a century, she thought, trying to allay an onslaught of fear. Something unearthly stirred in the room. She found herself reciting poetry in her head to calm herself. Never had stillness seemed so loud and menacing.

Robert Louis Stevenson's lines chanted rhythmically in her memory, keeping time with the wicked dance of the treetops outside which leaned toward Sheridan Road and the lake.

> ...*Whenever the wind is high,*
> *All night long in the dark and wet...*

She paused, flipping to another photo in the old file from 1908.

> *A man goes riding by.*
> *Late in the night when the fires are out,*
> *Why does he gallop and gallop about?*

Glenda didn't look up but she sensed another person's presence. It's just Helen, she thought. Yet in the dim library she felt transported, not elsewhere in the present, but back into the photo file, as if she were part of the black-and-white world of 1908 portrayed before her very eyes.

Am I going mad? Glenda wondered. Treetops scratched the windows like the bony fingers of some midnight specter. Suddenly she felt claustrophobic and, jumping up, she knocked over the rickety chair she'd been sitting in. It fell with a hollow thud that coincided with a violent crash of thunder from outside. Ugly feelings of agoraphobia, once familiar, hadn't attacked her in years. Yet now, all at once, she lost any logical hold she had on her whereabouts. She couldn't remember where she'd parked her car or which way she'd turn on Sheridan Road if she ever escaped this strange place. How to find her way back to Rosedale? Away from what used to be Northwestern's Music Library? This grand edifice had mysteriously metamorphosed into an alien place. Her eyes followed spiderlike grey and black shadows, tracing their paths up the walls. Fear. Loss. These unwelcome, intrusive apprehensions from her past flooded her psyche now. Although she fought the urge to gaze upon the dreaded photo again, her eyes were drawn to the file against her will, just as a child fights the urge to see the witch in the blackness of a bedroom mirror after lights out.

And although she'd pursued the truth behind Susan's murder fearlessly until now, all at once she doubted her own emotional stability in dealing with the demons she'd unwittingly unleashed. She could see Susan's slumped-over body in her mind's eye, her friend's blue skirt hiked up disturbingly high on her thighs, her light brown hair cascading down on the table. But somehow the harshest detail had been the sight of her friend's stiff grayish hand flat and immobile on the tabletop, next to her wine glass.

Had the jazz age pianist who'd pounded out the chords to the "Maple Leaf Rag" on the night of the murder, and the day before, been lying dormant for seventy-five years, just waiting for the proper channel in which to unlock a dimension and pounce on a guileless human?

The brown-out had deepened. Glenda could see only the white of the pages on Helen's desk, the dark volumes on the shelves, and the mahogany tabletops around her in the near-darkness. Holding the photo close to her eyes, she realized that a young woman in a high starched collar and black skirt looked startlingly familiar. If she could only identify the woman, maybe she could fill in details of the double murder of Doc Reilly and Rose Green, the two lovers from the Songbirds that Griz had described to Jack.

Rising, Glenda started toward the front desk.

"Excuse me?" she said blankly to the empty room. As she drew closer however, her pulse quickened. The desk looked to be in perfect order with only a small pile of Post-It notes on one corner. She tested a drawer, starting with the one Helen had retrieved the flashlight from, but found it locked. A computer sat on another corner of the desk. How had I not noticed that, she wondered? Then a whiff of lavender incense hit her nostrils and she stiffened, not daring to breathe.

What was going on?

Rain drummed on the windowsill. Stalking over to it, she pulled the window shut, then whipped around to face a blinding light directed straight at her.

"Thank God," Glenda said, stepping toward it. "I need to get out of here. There's a tornado coming and I'm nervous about finding my car. What happened to you? And where are all the students? Do you think the weather's scared them away?"

After an interminable silence, a male voice boomed.

"Who in blazes are you and how did you get in here?" it demanded.

Glenda stepped back in the darkness, backing up against another open window. "Helen, the librarian, helped me find a file I was looking for. She used her flashlight. I've been here since the library opened."

"What librarian?"

Glenda swallowed.

"The library isn't open yet," he said, flicking on an overhead light.

Glenda could see his blue uniform now, and his face looked irritated.

He shook his head, taking her by the arm and walking her to the door.

"I don't know who you are but you better get out of here now. This library has some valuable documents," he said, taking the file from her.

As he locked the door to the library, he shone the flashlight on a plaque indicating the library hours. "See here?" he said. "Open two to five on Sundays. The library doesn't open for three more hours."

Glenda blinked and followed him down the dark corridor. Descending the bleak stairs, her hand lingering on the gargoyle as they turned toward the foyer, she hugged her backpack to her chest, staring at the security guard's back in silence. But once in her Volvo, which she found as soon as her sense of direction returned, she pulled out the photo of the all-woman group she'd taken from the 1908 file. Under the heading "the Swallows of Chicago," she counted past four women in the front row to a smiling, tantalizing blonde, her head tilted in a mischievous expression. Lining it up with the corresponding name, she shuddered and counted again four more times. She felt certain the face was the same — the very face of the librarian who'd helped her. And sure enough, the name under the woman's picture read simply, "Helen Moss."

Chapter Eight

Many ideas and products improve with age; wine, quality antiques and rare manuscripts among them. Lucas MacDougal collected everything from Indiana farm machinery to Louis Vuitton luggage. A proverbial pack rat, Lucas MacDougal never discarded anything.

His rambling Queen Anne mansion, reminiscent of something out of a ghoulish movie, stood forbiddingly at the top of a hill at the end of Crabtree Lane in North Rosedale. The front yard stretched away to two acres down a hill, with a pond at the very bottom. The winters of Glenda Dominique's youth she'd spent skating the pond; in summer, she'd sit for hours with a stick and string, pretending to fish. The MacDougal property was a child's playground but only to those kids brave enough to venture near the place.

Lucas MacDougal filled the house with music, as his family had for a century; Lucas' mother, Ophelia, had favored Mozart, but Lucas forced Wagner and Stravinsky on the delicate ears of his discriminating family and friends.

Some time after 1915 the "Jazz Age," as F. Scott Fitzgerald once defined it, began, and the Lucas MacDougals never left it. Entering the mansion now, visitors would see a vast black and white tiled floor in the foyer. The tiles, cool under Lucas' feet in summer when he'd lumber in from playing his bassoon on the front lawn, displayed bass and treble clefs in relief. He'd had them embedded in the tiles when he'd inherited the house from his grandfather in the mid 1930s.

In Lucas' youth, his father, Siberius, a young, unusually wealthy musician for the early 1920s, played Dixieland jazz at his own wild bashes. While drinks and stock tips were passed around, Siberius and three fraternity brothers from Northwestern University would jam right there in the foyer. Tommy Smythe, the clarinetist, would get so over-zealous that his heel marks could still be seen on the white tiles.

Siberius encouraged parties — and trouble. He started the group tentatively called the Songbirds, changing it later to the Six Dixies. The sixth member would shake things up for generations to follow.

Siberius encouraged anything reckless, including bootlegging at the height of Prohibition. He fought all the temperance movements like the Right Worthy Grand Lodge of the Independent Order of Good Templars, the Women's Crusade, the WCTU, the Prohibition Party and the Inter-collegiate Prohibition Association, to name a few. Yet even while these anti-liquor movements boomed in the Midwest, so did Siberius' illicit liquor business.

Often the roaring parties at the Siberius MacDougal mansion would roll over to Cleary's Club on Lincoln Avenue on the near north side of Chicago, in the area known as Lincoln Park — now trendy and jammed with professional and artsy singles. In those days the area brimmed with speakeasies, jazz, and gangsters. Much of Chicago's reputation as a center of organized crime activity began during the celebrated days of ragtime pianist Scott Joplin and other famous jazz musicians and crooners. The rumors of the Biograph Theater where John Dillinger was betrayed by the lady in red to the FBI and police, and was gunned down as they emerged from a movie, have since become part of Chicago's infamous lore.

Siberius sank much of his fortune into buying Cleary's with Johnny Cleary, the pianist of the Six Dixies. Everyone who knew Johnny Cleary liked him, especially Rose Green, lead singer of the group. Rose had become the sixth member of the group in 1910.

Lucas MacDougal often found himself thinking of those days lately. Although only a young boy at the time, he'd heard about the murders of Rose Green and Doc Reilly his entire life. In fact he'd never lived them down. Somehow guilt plagued him, as if he were responsible. He'd devoted his entire life to proving Siberius' innocence in the scandal surrounding Johnny Cleary.

Now that he'd heard about the murder of Susan Sedgeway at Cleary's Club, he knew better than anyone that murder was nothing new to the club. It had been the scene of the other two murders back in 1920. The club had been an integral part of his life, and its legacy of violent death was part of the family curse, the family shame, the family secret. And only a few people ever acknowledged the hauntings that had plagued the club in years since the murders.

Now Lucas walked through the foyer and laid his bassoon down next to his banjo, clarinet, and tenor saxophone. He amazed fellow musicians with his ability to go from a stringed instrument to the double-reed bassoon to the single reeds of the clarinet and saxophone. He'd even taught other players of wind instruments the importance of soaking their reeds properly. Some rumored that he had more than water in those cups he always soaked his splintered reeds in.

Standing on the landing going up the vast staircase, he paused, pale hand to his chin. At the age of eighty-five, he no longer took the stairs two at a time as he had as a sprightly youth of fifteen on the many nights of notorious parties. The parties ended abruptly after Johnny, Siberius' business partner and friend, had been accused of double homicide in 1920. What happened after that no one dared discuss.

Something clattered in the hallway below and his heart skipped a beat. He's left Cleary's, he thought, and found me.

"Who's there?" he demanded, grasping his chest.

The creaking persisted. The steps sounded hollow, lifeless. The toes didn't touch the floor, he felt certain; in fact the feet seemed to scrape the wood, as if floating.

"I hear you, damn it! I know all about the girl Susan Sedgeway at Cleary's," he shrieked, pounding the bannister with his fist. "I know it was you and don't think I won't do something about it this time around. I don't care who thinks I'm mad. I won't let it happen again!"

"That you, Mr. MacDougal?"

The voice of Mandy, the housemaid echoed benignly in the hall.

"Who the hell's there? Damn you!"

Several rapid steps sounded, and the maid looked straight up to where Lucas clutched the white-painted bannister.

"Mr. MacDougal, please. You're not well. What are you doing up? You know what Doctor Patterson said. Get back to bed! What's that you're wearing? Oh, not again, Mr. MacDougal!"

Her voice dwindled from a scolding tone to sadness. She approached the stairs, one foot on the first step.

"Don't venture near me!" he said, smoothing his dusty black waistcoat.

Mandy shook her head, noting his use of archaic language.

It signified trouble. She knew the clothes well; the matching suit pants, the turned-up starched white collar and elaborately tied cravat characteristic of the early 1900's. Whenever Lucas' "demon recollections," as he called them, came back, he retreated to the attic and took up Siberius' musical instruments, clothes, mementos and letters. Never certain whether he was trying to prove or disprove his father's innocence of the crimes, Mandy had witnessed the transformation many times in the five years she'd worked for Lucas. But now the murder of Susan Sedgeway at Cleary's Club had sent him into a tailspin. At times like these, Mandy would observe her employer's pathological searchings into his family's past and his own soul with pity and wonder. She herself didn't know the truth about Siberius MacDougal and Johnny Cleary. The townspeople, of course, only thought they did.

Now Lucas trudged onward up the winding carpeted stairs while Mandy waited below. He studied the large square toes of his grandfather's shoes, which had been carefully preserved in a cedar trunk wrapped in layers of Scottish lace for decades. He knew she was watching him, but he didn't care. The murder of Susan Sedgeway surely proved some force was at work. That's why it happened at Cleary's, he mused distractedly as he reached the top of the stairs at last.

Approaching the door to the attic, he reached into his pockets — his father's pants pockets — and pulled out a large ring of keys. Looking to the left and right over his shoulders like a wary secret agent, he slipped a large silver key into the lock and opened the door. The room was a relic of another era. Paintings on the wall hung from ribbons, in the turn-of-the century style. His face somber, Lucas walked past a glass-front cabinet of leather-bound books, to an ornate oak library box. Opening it, he removed a packet of press clippings from the *Chicago Tribune* from 1908 and 1920. Then the sound of a car skidding into the circular gravel driveway below the window made him slam the book shut.

Moving as quickly as he could to the window, he peered down to the green grass, straining to see around the large weeping willow planted a century before. But the sky had grown too dark and the car had pulled in too far for him to see. He heard the sound of the doorbell and clattered down the stairs of the attic, locking the door behind him. Reaching the landing, he noticed Mandy in the foyer again.

"Not a word of this," he said to her tersely. "You must swear to me!"

Mandy's eyes looked pained. She worried about Lucas' heart. "You know how he feels about this," she said. "He won't like it. And he thought you'd turned over those keys. Why, if he even knew all the stuff you've kept over the years, there's no telling what he'd do."

"That's why it's not for you to say. I finally got him to move out. So pretend you don't know what I'm doing."

The doorbell rang again.

"It could be dangerous," she implored.

Lucas reached the final stair and paused to catch his breath. Behind him, the Victorian floral wallpaper peeled in the corners. The waning day left a trail of light across the paper, casting a half-shadow across Lucas' face. He looked chalky and worn.

"Nothing is more dangerous than trusting him," he said somberly.

The long tubular chimes from the doorbell swayed this time, the bell ringing twice, forcefully, angrily.

"Open the door," Lucas instructed, grasping his lapel, one foot turned out. "I'm ready."

Poised as if about to make a speech, he held his head high. Mandy crossed the foyer to the front door, took a breath, and swung it wide. Then her mouth dropped and she rushed forward.

"My God! What's happened?" she cried.

Young Jake MacDougal stood on the doorstep, holding up a young woman wearing a green striped dress. Her face was covered in bruises. She didn't look up, but studied the floor, her eyes averted. Lucas looked past his grandson, clad in a Northwestern University sweatshirt, to Jake's broken-down 1968 Mercedes in the drive.

"I got the photograph from that crazy Dominique woman," Jake said. "But be real, Lucas. You know if she sees it she'll make the same connections about your father as the cops did. I don't want anyone in town to know about it."

"Of course not," Lucas said obstinately. "The truth should be known."

"Don't start your insane talk again. Let's just keep the Cleary name clean. It's more than family honor. We'd lose whatever money we have left if news got out about Siberius' manic depression and what really happened after he was convicted of embezzlement, gambling, and helping Johnny Cleary after he murdered Doc and Rose."

"He didn't have a hand in it. And Johnny didn't murder those two. That's the point. And now it's much more important than just that."

Lucas stalked off to the parlor where Mandy had helped Jake lay the injured woman down.

"Don't you see," Lucas pleaded. "Now with that friend of Glenda Dominique's being murdered at the club, it's all starting again."

"Ghosts don't murder people, Lucas! Cut it out! Now help me take care of Pamela. Someone did a number on her. I can barely get her to tell me what happened."

Lucas walked past the couch over to the fireplace. Leaning on the mantel, he looked at Pamela in a vast tarnished mirror.

He had taken her in fifteen years before, when she was only thirteen, a runaway from an abusive home in Alabama. It hurt him now to see her like this, broken and bitter.

Mandy swabbed the cuts on Pamela's face with a damp cloth, dipping it in a silver basin by the couch. Pamela didn't speak but groaned several times, shaking her head back and forth.

Jake paced the floor, arms crossed over his chest. Tall and lean, with angular features, he resembled Lucas except for his younger, more muscular frame.

"Where did you find her?" Lucas managed.

"It was pathetic. She was wandering along Sheridan road in Evanston. I'd been called there by Globe Partners to check on a possible real estate deal in the area. She won't tell me where she was or who did this to her."

Lucas approached the young woman. Pamela Burke stared straight ahead, her green eyes hard. Her striped dress was caked in mud, with grass stains and splatters of blood here and there. Her once-elegant manicure now looked chipped and uneven, and her tanned hands were dirty.

"Come on, Pam," Jake demanded. "Tell us what happened. Who did this to you? Do we know him?"

She stared at nothing, her eyes fixed on several paintings piled on the floor around the fireplace. One painting in particular showed a woman's form, her face twisted in anguish. Jake followed her gaze.

When *are* you going to get rid of those dreadful Dali-esque paintings?" he asked. "They're damn depressing."

"Siberius, your grandfather, purchased those in the mid-nineteen twenties," Lucas sniffed haughtily. "They're valuable."

"Right, before the big crash. It was no skin off his nose back then. They're probably worthless!"

"I'm taking them into town this week to get them appraised."

"Fine. Look at the great luck I had at the North Kenwood Antique

Store! I even called ahead — and they'd already given away the one photograph no one else should ever have seen! And of all people, to that crazy Dominique woman!"

"Her name is Glenda, Glenda Morgan Dominique. Great girl. Rough family life. She ended up okay. She's very bright."

"And too nosy. That's probably why her friend was murdered. I'm sure it was just drugs. And then that damn Claudia person had to end up strangled not a month later. What does that tell you? They're a wild bunch. They're all into drugs," he finished, pouring himself a Scotch from a Waterford decanter.

"I've known Glenda a lot longer than you have. I think you're still smarting because she didn't return the feelings you had for her back in high school."

Jake slammed down his drink and shoved through a swinging door into the kitchen. Pamela Burke had fallen asleep on the couch. Mandy looked up at Lucas.

"Don't you think we should call a doctor, Mr. MacDougal? She's really beat up bad."

Lucas nodded and reached for a Gotham 1920s-style telephone next to a kerosene lamp. As he started to dial, however, the prongs of the phone were depressed by a forceful hand.

"What the hell are you doing?" Jake said, hand on the phone, his eyes blazing.

"She needs medical attention, you fool," Lucas said, his eyes earnest. "Don't take your anger at Glenda Dominique and Pamela's infidelities out on this woman's physical well-being. She could die. We don't know if she has internal injuries."

Jake turned away brusquely and stalked to the window, arms folded over his chest.

"She should have thought of that before she went back to him. What does it take for women like this? They ask for the abuse."

Mandy scowled. "That don't make it right. I know better. After I left my Jimmy, I went to a lot of meetings for battered wives. We don't deserve none of the treatment we put up with. To be plain honest, young Mr. MacDougal, you don't know what the hell you're talking about!"

With that, she stormed out of the room and fled up the main staircase in tears. Jake grinned sarcastically. Then he looked at Pamela and his face grew grim.

"What are we going to do with her?"

As they stared at the crumpled woman on the sofa, her eyes opened, looking changed. Jake set down the photograph he'd stolen from Glenda on the butler's table in front of the sofa. Sitting next to Pamela, he stroked her hair with deceptive tenderness.

"Come on now, Pammy," he said softly. "Jake's here. Tell me what happened. Who did this?"

Her eyes fluttered and at his touch, she flinched and pushed his hand away.

"It's okay, sweetie. It's me, Jake. Tell us what happened."

She squeezed her eyes shut as if in pain. Taking a deep breath, she opened her eyes, now welling with tears.

"The body. I saw her. I saw someone near her. I know if I just concentrate, I'll remember who it was. I have to get my thoughts together. But I'm afraid!"

With that, she stiffened suddenly, hands to her face, and cried out.

"What is it?" Lucas said, stumbling forward.

Jake had picked up the photograph he'd taken from Glenda and unwrapped it slowly. This would be the first opportunity he'd had to really take a look at it and study the members of the group. He knew the picture was damning and could not become public knowledge. Yet as he had done so, Pamela had sat up straight as if in a trance. Now she struggled for breath as if choking, her hands to her throat. Her eyes darted around the room as if she didn't know where she was, though this had once been her home. Her eyes went to the photograph and the expression of sheer terror that crossed her face made the hair stand up on the back of Lucas' neck.

Grabbing both sides of her head, she pulled at her hair, as if desperately trying to stop her mind. With a trembling finger, she pointed to the photo, then fell back on the sofa. Lucas touched her forehead and took her pulse.

"She's fainted," he said, looking at Jake. "And her pulse is dangerously slow."

Chapter Nine

"I have to see you."

"Words I thought I'd never hear," answered Griz, with exaggerated inflection. "This is a shocking but pleasant surprise."

Glenda held back. "It's not what you're thinking," she said. "I want answers."

"Still a mysterious woman, aren't you? I'd love to see you. Where do you want to meet?"

"The Coffee Depot, today," Glenda said.

"Near the practice rooms at Northwestern?"

"Yes. Across from the park."

"I have a master class at the community college. Incoming freshmen — my favorites, you know. Can we meet after eleven?"

"Fine." She could feel his smile through the telephone, and it incensed her.

"What could I have," he said, "that you so desperately need after all these years, my sweet Glenda?"

"Her."

"Her?"

"I want to know the reason for her fear. I saw you in Cleary's garden."

He was silent.

"Tell me about your demons, Griz. The rage is still festering, isn't it?"

"Then what were you," he retorted. "My demon lover?"

She could hear the sound of liquid pouring. She leaned forward in her prairie-style easy chair, pulling back a lace curtain from the living-room window. Her fastidious neighbor Herb was raking leaves across the street for the second time this week. It troubled her to talk to Griz, even on the telephone, even from this safe distance. How quickly their idyllic breezy walks along the lake in Evanston had turned to brutality and violence. Something sinister had been palpable even at the beginning, she thought.

"Just meet me," she managed to say.

"Will Jack know?"

"See you at eleven-thirty."

Driving to Evanston later, her old Volvo sputtering, the serenity of the affluent tree-lined streets almost lulled her into thinking Susan hadn't been murdered, that a party hadn't turned into a nightmare of questioning, that she'd not been stalked by ghosts for the last four days.

Within a block of the Coffee Depot, her pulse throbbed in her neck and arms. She prayed she'd beaten Griz there but spotted his wild mane of hair as soon as she entered. For a fleeting second, she understood why college women in his classes went for him like lambs to the slaughter. He stood up as she approached, pulling out the chair across from him.

"Not necessary," she said somberly, pulling her Irish sweater more tightly around her as she sat down. "No need for a charade. I know the real you."

His smooth smile faded.

"I also know you roughed up the woman in green, the blonde."

"What woman?" he said, lighting a cigarette carelessly.

Glenda pointed to a no-smoking sign on the wall and he stubbed the cigarette out roughly in a bread plate.

"Leo Cleary's party. I saw you beating up a young woman wearing a green dress. She's now missing. Tell me who she is and why you were trying to silence her. What's her connection to Leo Cleary?"

"Why should I?"

Glenda smirked. "If you won't, I'll be glad to gather witnesses who'll testify to your sadistic teaching methods. I'm not afraid of you any more." Yet even as she said this, her pounding heart gave her away. Could he sense her terror? "This woman knows something about Susan Sedgeway's murder at Cleary's Club," she said finally.

He chewed the straw from his soda pop, and Glenda recalled the Pepsi breakfasts he drank for hangovers.

"Why the hell would that girl know anything about this Susan person's murder?" he said.

"Because I saw her in both places. I saw her at the scene of both murders. No one else seemed to, but I did. Why is that?"

She's too flaky to help," he muttered under his breath.

"Then you **do** know her," Glenda said, nodding to the waitress for coffee when she strolled past.

Griz glared at Glenda, as if thrashing her with his eyes. "If we're talking about the same person, then the girl at the party in a blue dress was simply my date."

"Green dress."

"Green, blue. I don't remember. She left early."

"Because you beat her up. I witnessed the whole thing, Griz. You can't worm your way out of this one."

He leaned over the table and took her hand firmly in both of his. "Glenda, why are you imagining things again? Your psychiatrist isn't helping you? Is this a repeat of your fantasies about ghosts, like Cleary's Club?"

"How do you know about the ghost at Cleary's?"

"Everyone hears rumors, especially when they're about Glenda Dominique, the woman with a ready cause. And especially when she's claiming there are jazz-age goblins from seventy years ago playing the "Maple Leaf Rag."

Several women at the next table stopped talking and stared. Glenda clenched her teeth, determined not to let Griz see her inner torment. Then she smiled at him.

"I never told anyone the pianist played the 'Maple Leaf Rag.'"

He tightened his grip on her hands. At the same time, Glenda glanced outside and saw Jack walking across the street. He didn't look in their direction. Still, she scooted back in her seat and hid herself from view.

"Don't get involved in something that's over your head, Glenda dear," he snarled. "You will get hurt — permanently. Or maybe this time you'll stay in the sanitarium for good."

"If I survived you, I can take anything. You know Cleary and Manzetti pretty well. Tell me your relationship to them and to the woman in green. Remember, I know a lot about you."

"As I do you. Consider this an ex-lover's warning."

"Ex-lovers don't matter to me. All I care about is finding Susan's murderer. I know Cleary's party and the murder of Claudia in the garden have something to do with it. And your argument with the woman in green implicates you in some way."

"It doesn't matter," he said evenly, enunciating each word. "You have nothing to go on and nothing to show the police or anyone who'd be crazy enough to listen to you."

She held her breath, then leaned toward him. "And that's where you're wrong."

She thought of the cameo earrings and the photo of Cleary's where they showed up so clearly; and the women named Helen Moss and Rose Green. How she wished she still had the photograph! And what of the young man in the sweatshirt and his interest in the photo? She hadn't been able to see him clearly, but felt certain she knew him. Something about his brisk walk and long strides had been familiar.

As she thought these things, she watched a couple walking along the tree-lined sidewalk, heading toward the coffee shop. Griz shoved a stick of gum in his mouth and eyed her with a scowl.

"There was hardly any physical evidence at the site of the first murder," he said, his voice low. "The one at the club. And the only prints on the glass were the bartender's, the victim's and Tony Manzetti's. That has nothing to do with me."

"Yes. But they've questioned Tony Manzetti. He even has Jack as a witness, of all people. And Jack swears he walked with Tony to the bar and that Tony never put anything in the drinks. The initial hypothesis of the coroner was that Susan died from some sort of poison."

Still speaking, Glenda sat up as the couple she had been watching began to argue. Now they were right outside the window.

She listened attentively to Griz without taking her eyes off him, so he wouldn't follow her gaze. Immediately she recognized the young man in the sweatshirt who had stolen the photograph from

her: it was Jake MacDougal. Hadn't he asked her out many times in high school? The blonde in the green dress studied the sidewalk, oblivious to her surroundings, looking acquiescent and somber. Glenda had to look calm. She mustn't tip off Griz.

"What is it?" he said suddenly, his eyebrows raised. Then he looked outside. "What do you know, good old Pamela Burke. Now there's a head case," he said cynically.

"I just remembered, I have to go. Thanks for meeting me," she said, rising.

As she stood up, however, Pamela Burke peered into the coffee shop and upon seeing Griz, recoiled and stepped backward with her hands to her face. Jake supported her, but gave Griz a look. Griz, meanwhile, settled back in his seat.

Within seconds, Pamela had scurried across the street to the park. Jake stood by momentarily, perplexed, then raced after her amidst honking cars and traffic.

"How do you explain that?" Glenda asked pointedly.

"Don't know what you mean," he said, leaning forward from the shadows.

He grasped her hands in his again, his deep brown eyes full and intense. As she watched him, she felt a flicker of the passion they'd once inspired until she yanked her hands away forcibly.

"If you don't tell me who she is," she said, "I'm going to

the authorities at the junior college and you'll be run off campus, yet again, for sexual misconduct."

"And once again, you have no proof of anything," he said, his voice building. "Not of the murders, nor of anything else."

With that he tossed a tip on the table and stumbled outside. He stalked ahead of her as if she were importuning him for money, waving her comments away.

Soon they passed the aged practice buildings for the Northwestern University music students. The weather had warmed up, and some of the windows were thrown wide. The sounds of a 1940s-era ballad sung by a mellifluous soprano voice, drifted down to the sidewalk.

Glenda looked up, startled. She knew the song. Griz looked up too, unnerved, as if he knew the voice. Glenda saw the panic on his face as the strains of "What's New" filled the air.

Glenda searched the music building for the source of that lovely soprano voice. Then she saw the moon-shaped face of Miranda Gloucester, who was leaning languidly in a window. Seated next to her on the windowsill was Chick Natale, in opera-length pearls and a black dress with a high neckline, looking like some movie diva. She leaned back in the space of the window and stared straight at Glenda.

It's as if she's singling me out, thought Glenda, from other pedestrians, vagrants, bicyclists — and sex offenders. Why did she think that? Was Chick singling her out, or looking for Griz? Glenda couldn't be sure.

Regardless, Griz slowed down as the words carried from the depths of the soundproof room out to the street. Glenda recalled that around the turn of the century, the soundproofing of walls was accomplished with the use of seaweed. Perhaps for this reason, the melancholy voice reminded her of some long-dead sea nymph, mourning the loss of another whaling ship.

The words carried hauntingly:

"What's new?
How is the world treating you?
Handsome as ever...you haven't changed a bit,
I must admit.

In the background of the small practice room, Glenda could make out Miranda pacing back and forth, smoking a cigarette. Then Glenda turned and followed Griz's path.

"What is it, Griz?" Glenda said. "What do you hear?" But he did not answer.Glenda raced ahead of him and stopped him with a hand on his chest. The voice drifted after them:

What's new?
How did that romance come through?

We haven't met since then...
Gee, but it's nice to see you again.

"You're a crazy woman, Glenda," he said too loudly, as if trying to drown out the music. "You were crazy in college and obviously years of therapy haven't helped."

"Whatever you'd like to believe, Griz. But tell me this, why is there a trail of women following you wherever you go? What is Chick Natale singing? Is she sending you a message? Or is she trying to tell us something?"

Arms folded, Griz studied her coldly. Glenda felt that her knees would buckle, but she stood by resolutely. All at once, his expression softened and his wide mouth broke into a grin. Glenda was baffled until Griz stepped past her, his tone overly cordial.

"My dear Carolyn!"

Glenda whipped around to see the attractive and well-dressed Professor Carolyn Stind — whom she called the certified nympho-maniac for young male students — walk up. Accompanying Carolyn was a much older gentleman whom Glenda vaguely recognized. His posture was slightly stooped and his well-pressed but somewhat dusty clothes seemed to have come straight from a vintage shop on Clark Street.

"Hello, Gordon," Carolyn said, looking guarded.

"Please, it's Griz. You remember."

"Gordon," she continued, obliviously, "this is Lucas MacDougal. He's lecturing as guest speaker at two classes this week. He was once a professor of history here, if you recall."

She regarded Glenda suspiciously as she spoke. "Weren't you with that pleasant Jack Dominique the other night?"

Glenda smiled.

"I believe you played the clarinet at one time, too?" Lucas said.

"I did take a couple of master classes here at Northwestern one summer. In fact, I now teach private lessons out of my home, as well as owning an antique store here in town. But I graduated from the University of Illinois, Champaign."

"That's right," he said, nodding. "What's the name of your shop? Is it the little one with old books in the window and chintz curtains? A blue awning out front?"

"Yes," Glenda said, smiling. "It's a very old space. The name of the store is 'In Retrospect.'"

"That's right! How clever."

Carolyn tossed her hair over her shoulder flirtatiously. "Then you must have known Leo Cleary and Tony Manzetti when they were roommates at University of Illinois?" she said.

"I just learned about their acquaintance recently, actually," Glenda replied.

Griz shifted his weight uncomfortably from one hiking boot to another, hands shoved in the pockets of his baggy corduroys.

"So what's the lecture about?" Glenda asked, turning to Lucas.

"Good of you to ask, Glenda. I'm going to — that is, I'll be speaking about estate jewelry and vintage fountain pens. They are hobbies that an old man like myself can still enjoy."

"I'm sure it's of interest to many people, Lucas," Carolyn gushed. "Especially these kids on the North Shore. They're from families with money. That blue-blood wealth, you know."

She smiled in a deprecating way at Griz, who deliberately avoided her eyes. Glenda couldn't help but see Griz's notoriety as nothing more than a caricature. Only someone like Carolyn Stind would have failed to find his sexual appetite abusive, Glenda mused. Back in the seventies, the lists of Carolyn's conquests had once been rumored to rival the rosters of fraternities.

"What kind of jewelry will be on exhibit?" Glenda asked, turning to Lucas MacDougal.

"Art deco; some art nouveau. I have some real treasures — rare brooches and pins."

"And," prompted Glenda, "earrings?"

Griz watched her intently. Even Carolyn Stind seemed to feel an odd electricity.

Lucas MacDougal nodded.

"Oh, yes. Definitely earrings. Many have stories to tell!"

Glenda pulled Lucas aside, out of earshot of Griz and Carolyn.

"Well," she said, taking out a Polaroid of the drop cameo earrings she'd borrowed from Detective Halloran, "what story can you tell me about these earrings?"

Lucas' smile faded and he looked serious. "Where did you get that picture?"

"It's from a police investigation. I have friends on the force."

"Those two women recently murdered, I'll bet," Lucas mused. "Yes. I recognize the earrings. The design that is. They date from around 1918, 1920. The original pair was commissioned by Johnny Cleary, the former owner of the club for his lover, Rose Green."

Glenda nodded, jotting notes on a small pad.

"So as far as you know, you're not familiar with any local company who might have been replicating these earrings?"

"No," Lucas replied, hesitantly, then, "whoever it is, I wonder why they chose that exact design?"

Glenda shook his hand, "I'd like to find out," she said.

Griz and Carolyn still talked excitedly. Glenda raced off to her car.

Back at home twenty minutes later, Glenda phoned Detective Halloran at the North Kenwood Police Station. His secretary answered.

"Hi Stacy," she said. "Is Detective Halloran busy?"

"As usual Glenda. Can someone else help you?"

Glenda thought a moment. "Yes. Let me have Dan Schmidt. I knew him in college. He works in the basement next to forensics."

"Hold on, I'll transfer."

Minutes later, the call went through.

"Dan. It's Glenda Dominique. How have you been? I know it's been a while, but I need a favor. Could you get the earrings from the recent murders of those two young women? You know, Susan Sedgeway at Cleary's and the Reinert woman on the North Shore? They'd be in evidence or Halloran has them."

Glenda. I can't do that. They're part of an investigation."

"Tell Halloran it's for me. I just need you to read something off the back of them. Please Dan."

Two hours later, Glenda still paced the hardwood floors of her living room, waiting by the phone. Finally, the call came. it was Dan.

"All I can make out under the microscope here is "LT," he said. "Sorry Glen."

"No, thanks. Dan, that really helps."

Minutes later, she phoned Mindy at the antique store. "Look in the rolodex for all the jewelry retailers I have listed in there."

Glenda jotted down the numbers quickly, then phoned several in Chicago, New York and finally, Los Angeles. No one had heard of a company called simply "LT."

Chapter Ten

Glenda pushed open the thick wooden door with its glass panel reading "5th Precinct/North Kenwood Police" and charged past the desk sergeant and through a swinging door toward Detective Halloran's office. The precinct house had been built in 1920s art deco style after the first station burned down in 1919. Glenda thought of this in relation to Cleary's Club as she reached Halloran's door. The neighborhoods around Chicago had many examples of pre- and post-Victorian architecture visible side by side, as in the Lincoln Park area. Cleary's had fallen somewhere on the cusp; its older structure sometimes felt dank and ominous, making the feel of its Prohibition-era facade that much more enticing.

Walking past the secretary's desk, Glenda opened Halloran's door.

"Glenda, no!" said his secretary, Stacy, jumping up.

Glenda stormed into the dusty, plant-filled office, throwing the door wide. A middle-aged couple sat across from Detective Halloran, the woman dabbing at her eyes with a Kleenex.

"I'm so sorry," Glenda said, "I've not been thinking clearly. I'm sorry," she said again to the bereaved couple and quietly closed the door.

She sat in a chair across from Stacy, her face averted.

"Told you he was in a meeting," she said.

"I know."

Minutes later, she stood up when Detective Halloran emerged. "I'm feeling nuts," she whispered to him as the couple walked out. "I just need a favor."

He scrutinized her with a frown.

"Okay, a few favors," she said. "Please tell me what the result of the coroner's report on Susan was."

He hesitated. "Let me have Stacy delay the next appointment and

I'll get the blasted file. It's on my desk. Sit, relax a minute. Stacy," he said, pointing to his secretary, "get Glenda some coffee."

Stacy nodded and yanked at her pink miniskirt as she rose. She gave Glenda a sulky look and cracked her gum. Within seconds, Glenda had settled into an overstuffed chair across from Detective Halloran, patting the patched armrests.

"Here it is," he said, throwing the file open and scanning the report. "But first, tell me your guess."

"Susan died from a slow acting poison," Glenda said, somberly. "It could have been administered up to six hours before the time of death. She died, I would guess, around one- thirty in the morning, which means the poison could have been in her system since eight-thirty — right before show time and just after Jack and I arrived."

"That checks out with the report so far," Halloran said, nodding.

"What I can't figure," Glenda continued thoughtfully, "is who slipped her the deadly dose. My prime suspects, as far as I know, have alibis and witnesses. And I'm not sure how, but I know that Susan's death and the Claudia Reinert murder are connected somehow. Aside from the fact that both women overindulged in alcohol and other drugs, I know first-hand that Susan also believed in other types of spirits."

Detective Halloran grimaced. "Not ghosts? Were they witches or something? Is that what you're saying?"

"No. But I understand that Claudia Reinert had first-hand experience with apparitions in her family somewhere along the line."

"Great. I'm investigating the murders of two crackerjacks! But remember, I'm not in charge of the first case; it's not my jurisdiction. It's Detective O'Hara's, downtown. He's doing me a favor by letting me in on his information."

"Susan and Claudia are victims. And not necessarily crazy. And I appreciate what O'Hara's doing."

He frowned. "That's right, that's right. You believe in all that garbage too. So who are your suspects?"

She smiled. "Back to my assessments of Susan's murder. I think it was someone who knew her, someone close to her, who knew she drank."

"You mean someone who would know that something could be put in her drink without her noticing?"

"Maybe." Glenda stared at a Rockwell print of the boy reading the doctor's credentials on the wall before a shot in the behind. She wondered aloud, "Could it have been administered any other way?"

"Sure," he said. "In food. By injection too, I guess."

"Do we know her involvement with everyone at the club?"

"That's what I wanted to ask you. We've narrowed down the suspects to those present at the club and at the party at Cleary's house, where the Claudia girl was murdered."

"The 'girl' was thirty years old, Detective. About my age."

"Okay, woman. *You* know. We also found out that she was a fellow alumna of yours."

"She went to University of Illinois?" Glenda asked.

"And she was one of them club girls like you, you know — a three-triangle-club girl?"

"She was a Tri Delta? I joined for a short time, but wasn't very active. I was too busy with music and my antique collecting, which of course got me into amateur sleuthing."

"Even then, huh?"

Glenda smiled. "She must have joined after I left."

"Guess so."

"Well, I experienced Susan's other-worldly trials first-hand. Something happened to her when she went on a weekend retreat her senior year with some theater types. They were at a farm up in Wisconsin that was supposed to be haunted. She told me about it once."

"What theater types?"

"It was around the time she met Tony Manzetti and Leo Cleary. Cleary was in music school and Manzetti just hung out with him. Cleary had made several actress friends by that time, and of course Manzetti wanted to know any women Cleary attracted."

"Interesting. According to some of the guys on the force, a lot of the fruitcakes at the Cleary party were theater types. That explains that."

"Look, Halloran, I have to get to a lecture at Northwestern," said Glenda, rising.

"Continuing your education?" he asked.

"You might say that. It relates to that earring you found on Claudia's body when she was discovered. In fact, could I possibly get another Polaroid shot of it?"

"I guess. The press got hold of it already, anyway."

******

Half an hour later, Glenda raced across the parking lot toward Pick-Staiger Hall. Grabbing a pamphlet on the way in, she read about Lucas MacDougal's background. Following a long professorship at a university out East, when he'd left a trusted servant in charge of the MacDougal home and property, he had returned to Illinois and to Rosedale in the late 1970s, when Glenda was in high school with his grandson, Jake MacDougal.

Entering the lecture hall, she noticed Miranda and Chick seated in a row near the back, as if trying to go unobserved. Once seated, Glenda slunk down in her seat and searched the rest of the auditorium furtively. The lecture had already begun, and the dim light made it difficult to see.

Twenty minutes later, she turned to check out the exits and spotted Jake MacDougal and the missing witness, the woman Griz referred to as Pamela Burke. Somehow she'd have to keep an eye on them and take notes on the lecture at the same time. Nothing I haven't already done, she thought, thinking back to college days.

Lucas began to speak about the significance of estate jewelry.

"Sometimes," he said, "an ornament such as a locket or other jewelry, often bearing the art nouveau face of a woman, would be worn in times of mourning. Jewelry was often made from a woman's own hair, braided into wreaths which they displayed in glass cases." He held up a rectangular case with cloudy glass as he said this, "Women had quite a bit of hair, you know. And no hair dryers," he finished, chortling at his own humor.

"Of particular interest," he continued, "were the intaglios, which are the reverse of cameos. Instead of the external relief of a woman's face, they were inverse and likened to the face of a male roman gladiator. The cameos glorified the lovely visages of the young ladies of the time. These could be found on lockets, bracelets, rings, and earrings. The point is, jewelry was often an item of special significance in the art nouveau and deco periods, highly personal, much like the grand fountain pens of old — the Parkers, Schaeffers, Watermans, and Mont Blancs."

His lecture had digressed into other areas of jewelry expertise when Glenda spotted Jake and his companion leaving. Scribbling last-minute notes, she jumped up after them.

Once out the exit doors, she looked left and right. Clouds had gathered; a storm was moving in.

In the distance, she spotted the two ascending the stairs to the second-level parking, Jake's grip on the blonde still strong. Racing after them in the freezing rain, Glenda popped open a small travel umbrella and reached them just as Jake unlocked the doors of the old silver Mercedes.

"Jake," she said, yelling into the powerful wind off the lake. "Stop a minute. I must talk to you."

He turned his head sharply. "Get in the car," he ordered Pamela.

"What's her name?" Glenda said.

"What do you want?"

"I have a right to know who she is, Jake. And I can tell by her bruises that she's the one I saw getting roughed up at Cleary's party."

"Don't know what you're talking about, Morgan."

"Susan was my friend. I just want answers, damn it! And it's Dominique now."

"What does Susan have to do with Pamela seeing the body at Cleary's?"

"Then you admit it! Pamela is the woman in green. She has to tell me what she knows!"

The rain made Jake's hair stick to his forehead. He looked once again like the teenager Glenda had known in 1979. Then, all at once, a timid voice came from the passenger window.

"I'll talk to her, Jake. Let me talk to her."

"Shut up, Pamela. You don't know what you're doing."

"Maybe she can help us. I can't take the nightmares anymore."

"She'll meddle and screw everything up. For the last time, shut up!"

Glenda stepped up, rain dripping off the end of her nose. "Hello," she said, extending her hand. "I'm Glenda Morgan Dominique."

Pamela Burke unlocked the back door of the old car.

"Get in."

Jake grabbed Glenda's arm.

"You don't know what you're doing. She's not stable, for Christ's sake."

"I can handle people on my own."

She pulled free from him and got into the back seat. Rain drummed the top of the car like a tin can. The two women stared at one another curiously.

"I'm listening," Glenda said as Jake piled into the driver's seat.

"I'm Pamela Burke, Jake's sister."

Glenda looked puzzled.

"But I've known Jake for years, and..." Glenda said, looking from one to the other.

"Lucas took her in as a runaway when she was thirteen," Jake said matter-of-factly. "Kept it under wraps and all. She went away to a private school. She's a step-sister of sorts."

"And that's where I met Griz," she said, her head bowed.

"Then I was right about your knowing him. And Griz deniedit. I see he's still battering women as an after-dinner sport."

Pamela put a hand up to cover her eye.

"That's all right," Glenda said. "I witnessed the entire incident. I have to know what else you saw. Did you see the body?"

The woman was silent.

"Tell her, Pam," Jake said. "You've brought her into it this far."

"I saw Griz. And I saw the body from a distance. But it wasn't until you found it that I realized someone was dead and Griz could be the murderer. But there's nothing I can do, don't you see?"

"You have to tell the police what you know," Glenda said. "Whether he's innocent or guilty isn't for you to decide."

"She won't do it," Jake said, staring straight ahead contemptuously.

"Why not?" Glenda said.

Neither of the two spoke up. Finally, Pamela looked up, her purple and black eye looking more cavernous and sinister in the bleak, waning daylight.

"I'm scared to death. He's brutal and he doesn't care who he takes down to protect himself. He has a violent temper. You know that."

Glenda looked grim.

"I remember his anger. He starts out so charming and then moves in for the kill."

"Exactly," Pamela said, trembling. "You see, he's not the only one I saw."

She bowed her head again and started to sob. Jake shook his head and tapped the steering wheel impatiently.

"Someone else?" Glenda said earnestly, putting her arms around Pamela's heaving shoulders. "Did you see someone else?"

Jake let out a disgusted sigh and got out of the car. As he stalked off into the rain, Pamela spoke up.

"I saw some*thing*, not someone."

Glenda blinked without taking her eyes off Pamela's profile. At last, Pamela turned to face Glenda. "I saw the piano player. I saw the same ghost you did."

Chapter Eleven

A t the antique shop called "In Retrospect" which Glenda had just opened a year before in Rosedale, she and her assistant Mindy were examining recent finds. Glenda ripped through several shoeboxes full of items.

"You're wild today!" Mindy commented.

"I just can't get over the luck you had at the estate sales in Wooded Hills," Glenda said.

"Lot of filthy rich seniors dying off lately. I've never seen so much jewelry. I looked for what you wanted. And here's your picture back."

Glenda slipped it in her pocket and dug through a large box which she'd placed on top of a mahogany desk, scattered with early edition books and fountain pens.

"Looks like you succeeded with the old magazines too," she said. "Here's the *Saturday Evening Post*, *The New Yorker*, and *Vanity Fair*. That's what I want," she said, grabbing the last one.

"Why *Vanity Fair*?"

"Anything scandalous appeared in *Vanity Fair* first. The murders of Rose Green and Doc Reilly stirred up the music scene something fierce in the nineteen twenties."

Glenda rummaged like a squirrel — diligent, curious, determined. After a moment she stepped back, victorious, a colorful magazine clutched in one hand. Pulling several other magazines off the top, she tossed them on the desk.

"I'll have more time to look at these later," she said, setting the pile to the side of the desk. "Show me what you have. Where are the earrings like the one in the Polaroid?"

"You tell me," Mindy said, untying a purple ribbon from a tapestry design bag and pouring out the contents — a pile of cameos and black onyx. "I want to see what you think. I found intaglios, too."

"These are very similar," Glenda said, sifting through the pile on the table.

She arranged a group of caramel brown and marble-designed cameos in a straight line. They looked delicate, the profiles eggshell in color. Soon she zeroed in on two pairs of earrings. One set in particular caught her eye.

"This is almost it," she said, holding up one of the cameos. "But there was something about the pair Claudia wore, something distinctly different, something not quite right. See, look at this," she said, handing Mindy the Polaroid that Detective Halloran had provided.

The polaroid showed a dangling black cameo clutched in Claudia's grey, quite dead hand. The cameo face looked longingly at something. Claudia's fingers appeared frozen and too pale for the tan Glenda recalled her having had that night.

"There was something in the photo that Jake MacDougal stole from me and the earrings Rose Green wore, I'd swear they were identical to the ones Claudia had on. But there was something strange about them; they didn't match exactly. Good job on the jewelry anyway, Min."

Mindy nodded.

Glenda pushed a stack of books across the table. "Why don't you shelve some of these first editions while I look through the magazines," she said.

Unpacking the magazines carefully, Glenda placed copies of *The New Yorker* in one pile, *Saturday Evening Post* in another, and *Vanity Fair* in a third. She found four issues of *Vanity Fair* in all, three from 1925 and one from 1926. Flipping through the contents, she began to search through the three from 1925. Then her eyes lit up. The September 1925 issue featured an article entitled "Jazz and Desire: The True Tragedy of Rose Green and Johnny Cleary."

"My God," she said. "Here's a story about Johnny Cleary and Rose Green! This will explain a lot."

Mindy looked down from the moveable ladder propped against the bookshelves.

"Is that the jazz guy? Does he have anything to do with Cleary's Club on Lincoln Avenue? I love that place!"

"He has everything to do with it. This scandal sparked the popularity of the club."

She flipped through the article as she spoke.

"This is it," she said, turning to the first page of the article. Black and white portraits showed a somber Johnny Cleary seated at a black upright piano and an endearing Rose Green, her hair piled high with soft tendrils around her face and a tailored, lacy blouse that hung softly on her small shoulders.

"Tell me the story," Mindy said, gazing at the photos over her shoulder. "That Johnny Cleary was a looker, huh? Leo looks just like him."

Glenda looked at her. "You know Leo?"

"Sure. I was in music school at DePaul University when he was there in graduate school. All the music students hung out at Cleary's. All the female undergrads wanted Leo Cleary."

"Interesting. Things haven't changed much."

Glenda pored over the article again while Mindy shelved books. Several times, Glenda caught her breath, astounded at what she was reading, until at last she gasped aloud.

"What?" Mindy said, descending the ladder.

"It appears that the owner of the club at the time was Johnny Cleary. He was the star attraction with his piano playing. He was known as the 'rag man' for his 'vast repertoire of turn-of-the-century and popular rag tunes.' Then a rivalry broke out in early nineteen twenty-four when a new musician in town, Doc Reilly, began stealing the limelight and the attentions of Rose Green, the lead vocalist of the 'Six Dixies.' Doc Reilly came to Chicago and the Cleary Club as an unknown, but he had left behind a wild legacy in New Orleans. According to this article, they define 'wild' as involving numerous affairs with unseemly women and leaving the South amid dubious circumstances."

Glenda smiled, still scanning the article with her forefinger. Mindy plopped down on a camelback sofa, her eyes wide.

"Even by today's standards, this guy sounds like a real player, don't you think?" she said.

"But wait. It gets better," Glenda said, leaning back on the desk, still deep in the magazine. "Listen: 'The tragedy started when the skeletons from New Orleans followed Doc Reilly to Chicago. Some say Rose Green had agreed to marry Reilly but broke it off when she heard of his past. Some thought the rumors had been started by Cleary himself. Then, in a tragic twist of fate, Green and Reilly were found murdered. Johnny Cleary disappeared soon after and has not been seen in the Chicago area for over a year since the writing of this article.'"

Mindy sighed. "What a tangled web!"

The bell jingled over the front door; two customers entered and began to browse. The woman rubbed her arms in the chilly air that just ushered into the room. She was young and blonde, and looked preoccupied.

"Cold, isn't it?" Glenda said, amicably.

The woman nodded stiffly. "Indeed."

Half the time the blue-bloods of Rosedale didn't know who they snubbed anymore, Glenda mused, as she walked back to the desk and slid the magazine into a drawer. Looking up, she realized that the man with the rude woman was Griz. Her heart pounding, Glenda crept up the side stairs to the upper balcony. For ten minutes, she pretended to rearrange Depression-era glass while eavesdropping on the pair as they wandered below.

"What the hell are we doing here?" Griz snapped. "I've got to drop off this suit at the costume shop."

"I just want to look around," replied the woman. "This store's been open a year. It's known for its authenticity. In a couple minutes we'll go. Please, Griz?"

"I don't have time," he said, checking his bulky Rolex watch. "I told him I'd meet him at eleven."

Glenda thought he seemed nervous. How strange! Who could make Griz nervous, she wondered?

"Then go!" the woman blurted suddenly, stalking across a vast Oriental rug to a china cabinet. "He still runs you! He calls, you jump. How pathetic!"

"Keep your voice down!" he said, sputtering. "Do *not* embarrass me."

"I'm sorry. Calm down, Griz. We'll go if you want."

Glenda hid behind a cabinet of Wedgewood, her face anguished.

"Why do you annoy me? Have you forgotten what the doctor said about my stress level? You care only for yourself and I do everything for you," he said, taking a step toward her.

The young woman flinched, as if in dread of what would come next. Glenda recognized the fear, the passivity. As Griz drew closer to the woman, Glenda crept to the edge of the balcony. Grabbing a large volume of Shakespeare, she hurled it over the edge of the bannister just as Griz grabbed the woman's wrist. Glenda jumped back and listened as the book slammed to the floor. Griz had stepped away just in time.

"I knew it!" the woman exclaimed, her voice shrill. "I'd heard this place was haunted. They tried to tear it down a couple of years ago but some woman stopped the demolition."

"I know who," he said, angrily. "Glenda Morgan. Let's get the hell out of here."

He disappeared out the door, the front bell ringing an all-clear. The blonde woman stood in the corner and massaged her wrist. Glenda watched her over the railing as Mindy ran to her.

"Are you okay?" she asked, looking up to the balcony. "I don't know how that happened. The owner's particular about shelving books, especially heavier volumes."

The woman shoved her out of the way. "Let me out of here."

She grappled for the front door, and scurried after Griz. After several minutes, Glenda returned downstairs and retrieved the 1925 *Vanity Fair* from the drawer.

"It's criminal how fast he goes through women," Glenda commented.

"Who?"

"That was my old friend Griz. Remember the nightmarish relationship I had with him? I was all of twenty at the time."

"I didn't get a look at him but I could hear him all the way in back. Sounds like a nice guy. Does he rough up women for a living?"

"Looks that way. Unfortunately he now knows I own this place." She shook her head.

Mindy looked at her quizzically.

"Why would that matter?"

"He wouldn't have come in here if he'd known. Did you see how fast he cleared out? I overheard him say he was dropping off some sort of suit."

As she spoke, her eyes devoured the pages in search of the story. Then she saw another photo of Johnny Cleary. In this shot he wore a black tuxedo with tails hanging over the back of the stool. His black hair was slicked back with brilliantine. Glenda thought the smile on his face seemed all too familiar.

"My God, that's him," she said, her voice shaky. "That's the specter I saw. The one at the club the night Susan was murdered."

Mindy leaned over her shoulder. "That guy? Pretty good- looking for a ghost! I remember the night of Susan's murder — it sounded spooky. But you're sure about the details? I know you told the police and it's not that I'm doubting you, it just sounds so — *you* know."

"Crazy?"

"It must have happened exactly the way you said. That's what scares me."

"And...the day I got hit by that car in the alley? I heard him playing. I'm positive it was him."

As she spoke, she stepped to the window and gazed out across the street. She noticed Griz waiting in his red BMW.

"There *is* something about him," Mindy commented.

Glenda stared a moment longer, then turned to her.

"Who?"

"That Leo Cleary character. Granted, he always was a bit strange. And lately people have been talking. There've been a lot of rumors."

"What are you talking about?" asked Glenda.

"Well," Mindy said coyly, "I have a friend who used to go out with Cleary in college. We were in music school together at DePaul, remember?"

"What did you hear about him?" Glenda said, settling into a leather Victorian chair. "Let me guess — he has odd fetishes and a penchant for blondes. So what else is new?"

"He freaked out at a party once. Everyone thought he was on some sort of psychedelic drug until later on when we heard he said he'd had some sort of contact with the dead, some sort of supernatural connection."

"Psychedelics went out in the nineteen-eighties anyway."

"He had a strange effect on people, that's all I know. Especially women."

"Well, according to this," Glenda said, picking up the *Vanity Fair* again, "Johnny Cleary was high-strung and prone to periods of mania and severe depression, often in relation to his two major obsessions; jazz and women. The article goes on to describe the murders of Rose Green, the woman he loved, and his nemesis, Doc Reilly, the hot new musician in town."

Mindy started digging through another box. "And you said that Johnny Cleary ended up killing himself? See? Crazy behavior does run in the family."

"Actually," Glenda said, tracing the article with her finger, "there were signs that he'd intended to end it all, so they suspected suicide. In his journals they found the proverbial goodbye messages, entries showing that he'd planned on heading for the wilderness to die, where his remains would 'return to the earth' after he finished himself off."

"But they never found him?"

Glenda shook her head. "Or any clues to his whereabouts. And Rose Green was killed at the club by some strange method no one could explain. She just passed out during a performance."

Both women exchanged glances.

"How familiar," Glenda said.

They sat in thoughtful silence until Mindy spoke up.

"How did the Doc guy die?"

"That's another odd thing — he died the same way, on the same night."

"What happened?"

"He played the saxophone and the piano. That particular night, he was performing at Cleary's Club. There was a disagreement about who had rights to the club. You see, Cleary's was having financial problems. And Cleary's dad, a part-owner, had liked Doc's spirit, so in some verbal agreement over a card game, he had agreed to let Doc run the place. It was never put in writing."

Mindy shook her head, climbing up the moveable ladder again. "Wait a minute," Glenda said, scanning down the article with her finger. "It says traces of poison were found in the bodies of both victims — the same poison used in both cases, and assumed to have been administered in their drinks."

"Sounds like this Johnny Cleary had every reason to want to kill Doc Reilly. The guy was after his woman, his club, and the respect of Cleary's father."

"And all that was recovered from the 'suicide note' they found in his shabby apartment was a fragment that Cleary wrote. He said he 'would never rest in this life or any hereafter, until the Cleary name was cleared and the Club was safely back in the Cleary name.'"

Mindy stopped shelving. "What?"

Looking up from the magazine, Glenda grinned slyly.

"Don't tell me you're talking about ghosts again," Mindy said.

"No one can deny the two bodies that have turned up so far. And the first murder was a young woman at Cleary's Club, killed by a slow-acting poison, by my calculations."

"I don't get it. Who was Susan involved with — Tony Manzetti or Leo Cleary?"

"First it was Leo Cleary, then Tony Manzetti."

Mindy descended the ladder to greet a customer who was examining the jewelry counter at the front. On her way, she turned to

Glenda and whispered, "Seems like Leo Cleary has known every woman in town."

"It's true," responded Glenda. "But tell me more; you knew him in college."

As soon as the customer left the shop, Mindy settled into a needlepoint chair. "Rumor had it he was into weird stuff — the occult and getting in touch with spirits. Some say he was haunted by the whole history of his family."

Glenda smirked. "So you *do* know a bit about the family! What was your friend like, the one he dated?"

"She was a lot like what your friend Susan sounded like, you know — a wild partier. She had a lot of money, too, so much she didn't know what to do with it all. She and Cleary went on a lot of trips, and I don't mean in his car."

"He's an interesting character," Glenda mused.

"I think he's scary," Mindy said, her smile fading.

"Why do you say that?"

She hesitated. "I don't know if I can tell you. They say a girl killed herself because of him. But it turned out to be rumor. There was no girl at all, supposedly."

The doorbell jingled. "I'll take this one," said Mindy, jumping up to greet the young man who had just come in. But halfway to the entrance, she stopped. The two women stared.

"Is something wrong?" the young man said.

Mindy stuttered something unintelligible. Glenda stepped forward.

"You probably don't remember me," she said, hand extended. "I'm Glenda. This is my assistant, Mindy Mannion. Mindy," she said, turning to the stunned young woman, "this is Leo Cleary. Remember my telling you about his party?"

Chapter Twelve

L eo glanced at Mindy briefly, then studied Glenda, trying to recall her. He was dressed entirely in black, his curls pulled back in a ponytail, and wore a purple crystal around his neck on a black silk cord.

"Nice to meet you," he said to Mindy, then turned back to Glenda. "How are you since the other night? I'm sorry, I've forgotten your name."

So much for being memorable, thought Glenda, swallowing her pride. "Glenda Dominique."

"I guess you saw the unfortunate bit in the paper about the two murders," he said, holding out a *Chicago Sun-Times*. "They've gone to town as usual. It's brought the Cleary Club and all the old horror stories back into the limelight."

Glenda took the paper from him. She'd seen the article already but hadn't yet studied the photographs. On the left was a black and white portrait of Claudia Reinert, the woman Glenda had seen both at the club and at Leo's party just before her murder.

Probably a publicity still, Glenda mused. Then her heart jumped. In the photo, Claudia was wearing *the* earrings. Glenda felt sure they were identical to those her friend Susan had been wearing the night she'd been murdered. Again she noted the odd combination: one was a cameo, the other an intaglio. But now she noticed that when the earrings were worn properly, the man in the intaglio and the woman in the cameo seemed to stare at the same thing. Was this her imagination?

"Something seems very interesting to you," remarked Leo, pulling out a pack of cigarettes.

"Sorry, no smoking in the shop," Glenda said. "It's a fire hazard." She smiled, hoping the comment would deflect his curiosity about her fascination with the photograph of Claudia.

"So how is it bringing the club back into the limelight?" she said casually.

Leo browsed through the shop, touching a bronze sculpture of a young boy that stood next to a dresser. "My family has been through a lot over the years," he said, mysteriously. "And I had nothing to do with any of it."

Mindy settled into a chair by a dining-room set. "Nothing to do with what? The two murders?"

She laughed girlishly and looked over at Glenda. Glenda just shook her head. The powerful attraction that Leo Cleary seemed to exert over all women mystified her. What was it about him? she wondered.

"No," Leo said. "I never had anything to do with it — not then, not now."

With this, he wandered out of earshot. Had Glenda misheard him? As desperate as she felt to push the issue, a group of elderly women had wandered in and now walked about the shop. Glenda nodded to Mindy to wait on them.

Approaching Leo, Glenda stopped short when she caught him staring at her in the reflection of a tarnished mirror. His eyes were intent, but ambivalent, as if everything he'd ever said or represented as true now meant nothing. Who was he? She felt his presence was somehow otherworldly. She half-expected his reflection to disappear from the mirror like something out of a low-budget vampire film.

"What was that you just said?" she asked, able to reconnect her thoughts despite his theatrics.

"I'm innocent. So was he."

"What makes you think the police will believe you? You were incredibly calm at your party the other night, despite having just lost your ex-girlfriend only a month ago."

He wheeled around on her sharply.

"Are you calling me callous? Because to me that's worse than being called a murderer."

Glenda looked at the photo of Susan Sedgeway in the newspaper she held. It seemed inconceivable that one of her oldest friends, someone so young, had actually been murdered. But Susan didn't wear the earrings in the photo. It could have been an old college yearbook picture, the face was so cherubic — too young to have been so involved in pain and in drugs.

"I'm not accusing anyone just yet," Glenda said carefully.

"You were close, weren't you!" he said.

She glanced up and, for the first time, really looked him in the eyes. He still looked guarded and his expression was glazed.

"She had been one of my oldest friends. But frankly, in the past several years, she had changed from the young woman I knew in college and our sorority days. She went from being carefree and spontaneous to being an addict controlled by alcohol and drugs. They took over her life. There was no Susan left."

"Not the song and dance of the drugs took my friend away," he said sarcastically. "Look, she was always a crazy girl; she just got out of control. Hasn't anyone looked into the probability that she overdosed that night at the club?"

"They know it was poison," Glenda said. "The coroner's report confirmed that."

"Pretty wild trick for someone who was sitting at the table right next to you all night."

"Before, you said 'he' was innocent back then," Glenda said. "Who were you talking about? Your great-grandfather, Johnny Cleary?"

He smiled a sinister smile, one that had nothing to do with good cheer.

"You *have* been the busy amateur. Don't you have a business to run here?"

"How did you know I owned this shop?" she asked, somehow flattered.

"I know everything about everyone — especially those bold enough to make my parties."

"You don't come off as taking much interest in other people — unless they're female and gorgeous," she said.

"I know about you," he said. "Our families have known each other for centuries. But I was innocent then. And I'm innocent now."

Her expression didn't change.

"Never mind," he said, turning away. "This is very nice," he said, picking up an orange fountain pen. "I remember when it came out."

"That's an authentic Parker 'Big Red' from nineteen twenty-five," Glenda said. "Retails for about two hundred and fifty. If you like fountain pens, they're making a comeback."

"I knew they would."

Glenda bit her lip. More theatrics? Was he crazy or reincarnated?

Mindy had overheard the conversation and now looked confused.

"Well, this whole murder mess must not be too bad for your business at the club," she said cheerfully.

Glenda looked at her sternly. But the expression on Leo Cleary's face took both women by surprise. Glenda thought he looked betrayed.

"Is anything wrong?" Glenda said.

"You don't know what rumors can do. They ruined him, they ruined me. That's why we had to run. There was no suicide, like they say here," he said, poking a hole in the paper through the center of Susan's photo.

He turned and stalked out of the shop, hurling the paper angrily aside. Mindy picked it up and stared after him. Glenda swept past her, but Mindy took hold of her arm.

"Where are you going?"

"After him," Glenda said, grabbing her jacket from behind the door. "I have to see where he's going. Keep an eye on the shop."

"Glenda! He's dangerous. He may have murdered your friend Susan *and* Claudia Reinert."

Glenda had raced halfway down the block by the time Mindy blurted out her final admonitions. The shop was located at the outskirts of Rosedale, only a four-block jog from the elevated train. As Leo hopped a local train headed for Lincoln Park, Glenda followed, relieved that she'd pocketed some cash before running out of the shop.

Once on the train she walked briskly from car to car behind him, careful not to let Leo see her, staying close to the conductor and other passengers. Since it was not rush hour, the trains were nearly deserted. And Mindy had recently told her about off-hour attacks on college women on non-rush hour trains, even at nine o'clock in the morning.

Glenda's mind went back to Leo Cleary and the night of his unusual party. Claudia had indeed acted strangely, and her anger had been directed at Leo in particular. Glenda had to find out why Claudia had fingered those earrings over and over again. Was she signaling someone at the party, or was it just a nervous habit?

The train pulled up to the Clark and Lake stop and Glenda spotted Leo alighting. Within minutes he'd switched sides of the track and hopped a Ravenswood train. Glenda jumped onto the "A" train with him just as the doors closed.

In her haste she'd again boarded a half-empty car. Across from her sat two tough-looking youths, one chewing gum and staring at her, the other smoking a cigarette despite a "no smoking" sign.

Where are we going, she wondered? Then her mind returned to the party. Maybe if I figure out who was at both the Cleary Club on the night of Susan's murder and at Leo's party, I'll find a common denominator. She listed the characters in this double homicide play in her mind. Leo Cleary, of course; Jack, herself, Monty Simms; the club-owner; Chick Natale, theater student and aspiring actress; Miranda Gloucester, her fellow acting student and supposed part-time dress designer; Tony Manzetti of course, Leo's loyal follower as well as the business savvy behind Cleary's talent; and Claudia, who'd apparently been one of the peculiar set at the next table the night of Susan's murder, seated with Chick and Miranda. Having not known who they were at the time, Glenda had failed to account for them. Glenda also added Griz and Professor Carolyn Stind to her mental list, for Jack had informed her that he'd seen them at the club on the night of Susan's murder as well.

Now Glenda noticed a police officer seated at the other end of the car she rode in and sighed with relief. Suddenly she remembered that the same officer had shown up both at the club and at Cleary's house in North Kenwood. How strange, she thought, that he would turn up on the nights of both murders. Cleary's house was within the city jurisdiction, but Nelson had definitely worn a North Kenwood police uniform. A private cop, she wondered? Bodyguard? Or had Leo Cleary paid him off? What hold did Leo have over everyone who knew him?

The train jerked suddenly. The cop eyed her as the train screeched up to the Fullerton stop. Glenda looked out the window, crouched in her seat. Leo went quickly past, trying to appear casual.

Glenda smiled sweetly at the cop, then jumped up before he had a chance to react and yanked down on the emergency lever. She didn't want this policeman involved for now and managed to leap out the doors just before they slammed shut.

She followed Leo past Bissell, off Sheffield, until Leo crossed the archaic and grandiose DePaul University campus, heading toward the music school. He whipped through revolving doors of the sixties-style music building, which looked odd next to a picturesque white-steepled church. Glenda knew the campus, for she used to attend music concerts of her friends at DePaul's music school years before.

Glenda waited a safe four minutes after Leo had disappeared

before descending the shallow stone steps. Looking left and right, she logged herself into an apparent "practice room" ledger and waited for any student to approach.

"Can you help me? I've forgotten my pass," she said coyly when a sandy-haired young man walked up carrying a tuba. "I'm a voice major. If I don't practice my arpeggios for my scholarship audition tomorrow, I'm sunk."

He smiled, reaching for his pass, then hesitated.

"Isn't it a bit late in the quarter to audition for a scholarship? I thought they were already awarded."

Glenda rolled her eyes sheepishly.

"What can I say? You know how absent-minded musicians are!"

He laughed knowingly. Glenda felt guilty for admiring the fit of his university sweatshirt. The hall monitor had left the desk outside the practice rooms so the young man inserted his card in an electronic slot next to the locked doors.

Once inside the maze of practice rooms, she felt a flicker of old guilt. She'd never practiced, yet always done well in music school. Sounds of an oboe cut through other instruments in an alto, melodic strain; a piano practiced scales up and down and a tenor voice sang "I'm a Yankee Doodle Dandy." But it was the broad, manic chords of the "Maple Leaf Rag" that made her heart skip a beat. She hadn't lost Leo.

Following the twists and turns of the passageway among soundproof rooms, each with large glass windows, she traced the sounds of the jazz piano, her whole body trembling with anxiety. Some odd force spurred her on, however, and she felt driven to continue, unable to stop herself. Suddenly she paused at a corner where a clarinetist played Mozart behind her and a trombone slid through scales in the room opposite. Yet through both, she could hear the "Maple Leaf Rag" played with a sinister taunting insistence.

The air felt heavy. Glenda struggled to breathe naturally. Turning several times in place, she wiped her forehead. All at once, panic overtook her and she felt an urgent need to get out of the place. She knocked on several practice room doors but could gain no one's attention. She ran from door to door, gasping as if the oxygen had been shut off.

Damn this soundproof glass! she thought, panicked.

Although she could hear her own knocking, all the music students were totally engrossed in the pursuit of their craft.

The lights within each practice room shone brightly. But then the hall lights seemed to dim. Glenda raced down a hallway and tripped. Amidst the din, the "Maple Leaf Rag" pounded and pounded, resounding in her ears like a gong.

Picking another practice room door at random, she knocked again, her eyes averted. Then she saw him.

Leo Cleary leaned forward into the keyboard, thumping out the chords to the "Maple Leaf Rag" over and over, as if in a ritual. Glenda noticed, with some horror, the beads of sweat at the sides of his temples, his hair looking twice as curly as before and now freed from its ponytail.His shoulders heaved as he raced up and down the keyboard with agile fingers, seeming not to play but to be a part of the piano somehow. It was a violent interplay, practically sexual in magnetism. But his expression made her feel faint.

His face was pasty white and his eyes looked askew, as if staring into another dimension, a world visible only to him. Glenda realized she must not let him see her. Then, without warning, he slammed both hands flat on the keyboard and his head snapped unnaturally to the right like some kind of android, catching her off guard in his alien stare.

Chapter Thirteen

Suddenly two firm hands grasped her shoulders from behind, yanking her to the exit doors of the practice rooms.

"What's going on?" she said, turning her head to see the sandy-haired tuba player.

"It's a tornado warning, we're having a brown-out. That's why the lights dimmed. We go to the basement."

Glenda freed herself and faced him. "What about that piano player? Do you know him?"

The young man pushed her along with him gently, down concrete hallways that looked as if they had been built in the 1960s, until they reached an older underground area where students and professors had gathered. Some chatted, some studied, some just waited calmly.

"Well?" Glenda persisted. "Do you know who I mean?"

"No. The only pianist practicing today, according to the log, is my girlfriend Jan. I know that for sure 'cause I checked to see if she was here today."

Glenda's mind worked rapidly.

"Have you ever heard of Leo Cleary?'" she asked.

He laughed.

"Who hasn't? The guy was a legend here — for his music and his women." The young man set down his tuba and leaned back on a formica table. "You know who knows a lot is that speaker, that older guy, Lucas MacDougal. He knows a lot about the Cleary name. I'd be careful who you run into though."

"Why?"

"Pinehurst, the mob — you know. It's all rumors. But they say the Cleary name, the town of Pinehurst, and the Mafia have gone hand in hand since Prohibition. This *is* Chicago, right?"

He chuckled. Glenda nodded absently, forcing a smile. She'd spent four years in Champaign, Illinois explaining to the locals there that Chicago was no longer the town of machine guns and gangsters in every movie theater.

"You mean that even today, Leo Cleary has connections to the mob?"

"That's the rumor. Lot of students hang out at the club to see Leo play. The music students bring their instruments and jam with him. He's cool."

Glenda stood up from the table where they'd been sitting.

"I've got to get out of here. Doesn't that MacDougal character live nearby somewhere?"

The youth studied her, apparently reciprocating her earlier admiration of him. He looked her up and down several times.

"I can show you," he said. "Soon as the tornado drill's over. Someone has a radio around here. They'll sound the all clear and then we can go."

******

Forty minutes later, they were walking amid shadows and ivy along the private streets beyond DePaul University's music school, as other music students dispersed around them. A young couple kissed on a curb, their backpacks strewn on either side of them.

Glenda walked alongside the handsome musician. She still looked left and right though, as if expecting to see the elusive Cleary. As they neared a red brick dormitory, the youth suddenly stopped at the wall and blocked Glenda's way.

"My friend has a room here. You interested?"

Either despite of, or because of, his good looks, his youth, and her own subliminal desires, she burst out laughing.

"Look. You're misunderstanding me, buddy."

"Jeremy. Call me Jeremy."

"For one thing, Jeremy, I'm married."

"Happily?"

"I really need to see Lucas MacDougal. I've met him and heard him lecture. This is no fraternity bash. A good friend of mine was murdered at Cleary's Club several weeks ago."

"Man. I'm sorry."

"Beyond that, I need to know the history of the club," she hesitated, studying his reaction. "You know, if there were any strange stories relating to ghosts or odd legends that the club was known for."

He looked uncomfortable. His youthful smile warped all at once into a grimace.

"Yeah. There were a lot of stories. At first they gave the club a sort of notoriety, you know, spiced things up a bit. Sometimes it was a good way to get a date, you know? Tell 'em you're going to take them to a real like legendary spot in old Chi-town? Especially the farm girls from southern Illinois and Iowa — they kind of go for the jazz men and the music school scene. But then, well, someone crossed Cleary once. That's when things got really spooky. There was this girl, a young voice major. Cleary liked her."

"What happened?"

"Well, she didn't act the way Leo wanted her to. And things turned out pretty damn ugly."

"How so?"

"She was supposed to sing with his group one night..."

As Jeremy spoke, several music students strolled past. One couple was absorbed in passionate conversation; the man talked, his palms skyward as he stressed a crucial argument. They were oblivious of Jeremy and Glenda, yet Jeremy still seemed hesitant. He leaned forward and whispered to Glenda like a conspirator.

"He liked to play up the whole Johnny Cleary mystique. And then he got mad at this girl. Combine his theatrics with her blowing him off for another guy..."

"I take it she didn't sing?"

"She got to the club late. Leo likes to start on time. He's a stickler for punctuality. And he heard she was late because of some greasy long-haired drama major. So he pulled the Johnny Cleary routine to freak her out. Unfortunately, he didn't know she was so susceptible to suggestion, I guess you could say, or that she believed in all that Ouija-board crap."

Glenda leaned back against the steps where they sat and the youth smiled.

"What happened?" she asked.

"Well," he whispered, confidentially. "She freaked so bad that she had to take a quarter off from school."

"He was that convincing? How could that be?"

"My personal opinion? Because the guy believes it, that's why."

"What do you mean?" Glenda said, cautiously. "He thinks he's reincarnated?"

"It's a known fact that he's into the supernatural stuff. I was there.

He was pretty damn scary."

Suddenly another buzzing alarm went off. Glenda jumped.

"Don't worry," he said, hand on her shoulder. "That's just a second bell to sound the all clear."

Students began to file past Glenda and Jeremy. She stared at him expectantly. He kicked at dry leaves on the street.

"Go on," she said, gathering her composure. "Please tell me what you saw."

"You'll think I'm nuts."

She thought back to the ghoulish details of the night Susan was murdered and the strange trio of women — Chick, Miranda, and Pamela — so absorbed in their own dark, somber worlds that they were oblivious to the death of another human being at the next table. And yet she herself had been sitting right next to Susan and hadn't noticed anything. Perhaps that's what bothered her now.

"No," she said, shaking her head. "I won't think you're nuts. No one believes me either."

"Okay. It started out like any beautiful night of jazz, you know? Then this Cleary guy just sort of changed! But at the same time, the whole room changed. Like there were cold drafts everywhere. And it smelled like that bath stuff, like scented candles."

"Incense?"

"Yeah!"

"Go on."

"Well, let's see," he said, noticing her reaction with interest. "I think the floor felt gritty or something. And the room had turned light purple, no, lavender. See, I knew you'd think I was nuts."

But Glenda stared straight ahead to a neat row of brownstones. A thirty-something mother pushing a baby in a shaded stroller watched them. Glenda shook her head slowly.

"I don't think you're nuts. If you are, then I am too. Did anyone else see this transformation? And did anyone find anything afterwards, you know, like tangible signs of some sort of theatrics?"

"That's the thing," he said, his voice low as he looked down the street behind her. "The only other witnesses were a couple of other music students — some of Cleary's groupies, I figure. But they seemed kind of wasted, you know, partied out."

"What did they look like?"

"I don't know. It was dark and I didn't pay attention —except for one babe. I remember she wore a black dress slit really high on the side. Now *that* I wouldn't forget."

He smiled brashly.

Pamela, Glenda thought. Pamela Burke was there on other nights when Leo did his Johnny Cleary routine, when the ghost appeared. Does she know it's a routine? If so, then why did she tell me she had seen a ghost? Glenda started to walk again, deep in thought.

"I guess you'd better get me to MacDougal's house. I have a lot of work ahead of me."

"It's a couple of blocks," he said, catching up to her and pointing straight ahead. "We have to hop the el train to the north side of town. He lives on the outskirts of Rosedale."

They walked along like any other young couple, except their minds were filled with jazz clubs and apparitions. Neither spoke. Once off the train twenty minutes later, they approached an ivy-arched entrance to the mammoth Queen Anne mansion that belonged to Lucas MacDougal.

In front of the house, Jeremy froze.

"I'll leave you here," he said, stiffly.

"Aren't you coming in? I'm sure he'd like to see you again. Didn't you have him for some classes at DePaul?"

"Yes, when he guest lectured a few times," he said. "Look I don't know if it's true but it's been rumored MacDougal is a little beyond eccentric, kind of crazy and prone to wild outbursts. I'd rather drop you here, okay? I have to be somewhere anyway."

With that the tall, lithe Jeremy hurried off. Glenda stood by a moment, looking up the hill to the foreboding mansion.

Its blackish pines loomed over spires and dormers; the entrance was dark and menacing. Determined, Glenda squared her shoulders and started up the walkway.

She pressed the doorbell, humming along with the chime, fingering the Polaroid picture of the earrings in her pocket as she waited. After what seemed an interminable time, the door creaked open heavily. In the doorway stood Pamela Burke, wide-eyed and wan.

"Glenda?"

"Pamela. I'm glad to see you. I need some information."

"You're here to see Jake?"

She seemed, naturally, incredulous.

"No, Lucas. I need some history lessons about the Chicago area, especially the Rosedale and Pinehurst mob connections."

Pamela frowned. "Talk to Griz."

"Why do you say that?"

The young woman seemed to recoil, then remember her manners. "Come in, won't you?" she said, opening the door wide to reveal a high-ceilinged hall lit by a chandelier.

Glenda followed Pamela into a large parlor to the left, a plush burgundy Oriental rug feeling cushy under her feet. She settled onto a silk-upholstered sofa.

"I'll get some tea," Pamela said, disappearing down a long creaking corridor.

Glenda started, caught her reflection in a massive age-tarnished mirror. She hid her awe at the impressive collection of antiques and early twentieth-century art objects packed into the room. Turning around, she gasped suddenly at the sight of a stuffed grizzly bear standing on its hind legs, forepaws reaching out as if to attack. It reminded her of another predator just as Pamela returned with the tea.

"What about Griz and the mob?" she said.

The teacups on the tray clanked as Pamela set them down shakily. Her hands trembled as she poured hot water from a porcelain pot.

"I shouldn't have said anything," she said.

"Maybe you really want me to know. Come on, we both know all the illegal garbage the good Professor Griz is involved in. What's his connection?"

"It's his friends at Cleary's."

"So they're involved?"

"They have been for years. I'd heard that the mob has been connected to Cleary's since the days of Al Capone. Not at that level, but shady characters let's just say."

"I need to talk to Lucas. Is he here?"

"He's working in the basement." She smiled warmly. "He loves tinkering....It's been so different to know a kind father — that's not what I came from. You know he took me in as a runaway when I was only thirteen, even though it was kind of hushed up."

Glenda thought of Griz. Objectively, she could see this poor wretch's attraction to his abuses. But why had she herself fallen into it?

"Let me see if Lucas can come up," Pamela said then, rising.

Glenda walked casually around the room, noting photographs on tabletops and several on top of a black grand piano. To piece together the significance of the earrings worn by both Susan and Claudia, and their connection with Cleary's Club, seemed more crucial than ever. Just as she turned at the sound of approaching steps, she spotted a photo of a large Tudor mansion. Could it be? she thought. Quickly she yanked the polaroid of the earrings out of her purse. Examining the photo on the piano, she saw that it showed two stone statues in front of the Tudor house: a man and a woman, each in profile, looking toward the entrance to the house from opposite sides. There was no mistaking that they were the same images as those on the cameo and intaglio earrings in the police photo. The earrings represented this house, she thought. But why?

Sounds of heavy steps came from the pantry. Lucas clomped up the stairs, fifties-style black bifocals perched on the tip of his nose. He looked like an aged Buddy Holly.

"Who's there?" he demanded, barging into the parlor. He wore a flannel robe over a tattered pair of Oshkosh farmer's overalls.

Glenda stepped backward and shoved the photo in her pocket.

"We met briefly once or twice before," she said, extending her hand. "I'm Glenda Morgan Dominique."

"Right. Glenda," he said, gruffly. "I don't have anything to sell, if that's what you want."

Taken aback, she looked at Pamela.

"Calm yourself, Lucas," Pamela said. "That's not why she's here. She'd just like to ask you some questions."

"First off," Glenda said, showing him the photo from the piano. "Where is this house located — and whose is it?"

Lucas looked startled.

"That's just some old mansion in Pinehurst. I picked up the picture at a garage sale back in the forties. I just always liked the architecture, that's all. That's why I saved it."

Clearly, he wasn't telling the truth; Glenda could see that. But why lie? Who was he protecting? Just then the front door swung open and Jake plodded in, carrying several grocery bags.

"Pamela? Give me a hand here."

Upon seeing Glenda, he stopped short. He looked at the black and white photo in her hands. Although he didn't move, Glenda saw the apprehension in his eyes.

"How are you, Glenda?" he said, pleasantly. "What brings you here?"

"Visiting your grandfather. In fact, do you mind if I borrow him for the afternoon? That is, if it's all right with you, Mr. MacDougal."

She turned back to the older gentleman as she set the photo down on the piano again. Ten minutes later, after Lucas had gone to change and Glenda had offered assistance with the grocery bags, she peered into the parlor in time to see Jake raise the lid of the piano bench and slip the photo out of sight. By the time he straightened up to check whether anyone had seen him, Glenda had slipped back into the kitchen.

Chapter Fourteen

"So you don't believe me?" Glenda asked Jack, incredulous.

"Glen, you have to admit. It sounds farfetched. A librarian's desk converts to a modern one, she disappears, and a convenient storm hits making the whole scene something out of a horror movie."

He looked at her carefully. A question was forming.

"So you don't believe me?" she repeated.

"Have you relapsed?"

"What?" she sat up straight at the kitchen table and set down her coffee. "As in drinking again?"

"Are you drinking again?"

"You're as bad as the police. You know me better than that."

"I thought I did," he said, rising and walking to a bay window.

Glenda shook her head, her mouth agape.

"I saw you at the diner with Griz. What were you doing with him?"

"I was working on the case of Susan's death."

He turned to face her suddenly.

"I know what he's like. You two drank together years ago. That's what you told me. And that's all you said it was. Now I'm not so sure."

"You think just because I met with him I'm using alcohol again?"

"And you two were mighty chummy at Cleary's party. Didn't look like casual conversation to me."

She was silent.

"We were involved at one time."

"How involved?"

"We were lovers. I was a different person then. I was attracted to abusive types. But I swear to you, I'm not drinking again. I just needed information from him."

He nodded sullenly.

"I have to go," she said quickly. "I'm meeting Lucas."

Forty minutes later, they walked along the beach of Lake Michigan, the horizon slate blue and cool grey, just down from the Baha'i Temple in Wilmette. Lucas ignored his straggly grey hair as it blew in the relentless wind. He looked preoccupied.

"Why did you want to see me?" he asked finally.

"I'll get right to the point. I want to know about Rose Green and Johnny Cleary."

Lucas looked taken aback but didn't slow his pace.

"We've known the family for years. But why would you want to know about them? My God! Hasn't the Cleary name suffered enough? First Pamela is harassed and now this."

"Harassed by whom? By Cleary?"

"That Griz character. He beat her up! She told me all about the ghost she says she saw at the party, just before a horrible argument with Griz. I was a very young man in the days of the Johnny Cleary scandal. Sure, I remember Rose Green.   Quite a stunner, that one."

"Tell me again how it all happened. You know, the scandal at the club. I'm assuming there was involvement in bootlegging and I know that somehow the Mafia cornered the market."

Lucas turned on her. "Who wouldn't be involved in those days? In nineteen twenty-eight, everyone wanted to make it big. I guess people figured if a cartoon rodent like Mickey Mouse could make it, anyone could have the good life. Difference was, some people turned to the illegal way of doing it instead of straight show business. Now my father Siberius, he was respectable." He paused, his head bowed. "But he'd have done anything for his friend Johnny. It brought him down. He lost everything."

Glenda nodded. "Go on," she said, softly.

"The clubs were competitive. And at that time, the mob ran Chicago. I'll never forget the summer some of the lesser-known bosses were hiding out. We were staying at the same cabin."

"Lesser known bosses?"

"I mean the small crime hoods, friends of Cleary's who paid their dues to keep their clubs going to the more notorious mob bosses, but otherwise avoided all other contact with them. So these lesser-known thugs kept business going for Cleary, you know, hired musicians, kept the revenue coming in, most times with deals under the table, paying off cops. Stuff like that."

"And Rose Green?"

"Rose was a gem, but she had a fiery temper and she loved to drink. Anyway, in the beginning it was her and Johnny Cleary all the way — they were lovebirds, always together, performing their music and bringing in the crowds. But then the club started having cash-flow problems, and daddy Jeremiah Cleary told Johnny he had to bring in more business. That's about when Doc Reilly came on the scene."

"How was he involved?"

Lucas smiled. "He had bright ideas about how to save the business and make profits, and Jeremiah Cleary loved him for that." Lucas paused and lowered his voice. "Scary thing though, was that his connections included some questionable characters from Elmwood Park and Berwyn, some from Pinehurst too."

Glenda pondered this information. "Pinehurst is pretty pricey."

"Some powerful types came out of there. Now Johnny fought his father on this and they got into some terrible brawls — physical and all. And then to top it off Rose decided she liked Doc Reilly, and they started keeping company. So not only did daddy Jeremiah Cleary like Reilly, so did Johnny's girl. He was losing everything. Right after all these troubles began, Doc Reilly and Rose were found murdered."

He walked on ahead to the parking area off the beach. Glenda jotted notes on a steno pad, then stopped and looked squarely at Lucas.

"You're not telling me everything. I know there's more."

Lucas tugged at his starched white shirt under the black overcoat. He looked like the headmaster of some private academy.

"What do you mean?"

"Shortly after, Johnny supposedly disappeared, and it wasn't long before the club was plagued with hauntings. Although they never found a body, it was rumored that he'd killed himself. Isn't that right? Nearly ruined the business. They said his ghost was out to destroy his father's business for not being loyal to him, and that Johnny killed himself out of guilt for murdering Rose and Reilly. His soul couldn't rest."

"Yes," he mumbled, then repeated. "Yes!"

"So what else, in addition to what you told me that day outside the diner, can you tell me about these earrings?" she said, whipping out the Polaroid she'd shown him once before.

Although unflinching, his face revealed some fear, as if he'd hoped never to see the photo again.

"What about the images on them?" Glenda demanded.

"Let me see," he said. "Yes, the earrings I recognize, and I guess the images on them definitely are familiar as well."

"They should be. They're part of a black and white photo of some mansion in your living room. And for some reason, Jake put that photo away when he thought I was in the kitchen. What's he trying to hide?"

Lucas shook his head in disbelief.

"I feared the Wisconsin connection would come out eventually. That's what he's afraid of — that people will find out."

"Find out what?"

Lucas stood with his back to her, hands on his hips. He gazed toward the Baha'i Temple, as if in need of spiritual guidance.

"They fled. They all ran from the Pinehurst connection. The house belongs to the Cleary family. They were mob-connected. Jake figured you'd recognize the house, being the architectural expert he knows you to be: and, as I'm sure you've already heard from local folklore, the mob kept Cleary's Club going during Prohibition. The connection stuck all these years. But Leo resents the rumors. Lots of folks doubt Leo's stability. He thinks the whole Johnny Cleary mysticism is for real. It's rumored that not only does Johnny make regular appearances at Cleary's Club, but also that he speaks through Leo."

"So Leo believes he's the reincarnated Johnny?" Glenda asked.

"Or like some spiritual conduit. Anyway, Leo wants to clear the family name by proving that his great-grandfather had nothing to do with the murders."

"How?"

"I'm not sure. He's been seen doing a lot of research around town and at the Newberry Library. He's also asking questions of a lot of old-timers."

"What does all this have to do with Wisconsin?"

"Jake and I are worried about Pamela and what she knows. Leo Cleary is out of control and Griz knows the gang well. Because of her involvement with Griz, we're just worried that some of the underworld might decide she'd be better off dead. I know Griz is a fellow academician, but he's ruthless. He'd act like a hit man. Wisconsin is key because when I was a boy, and Johnny and his friends fled to Little Star Lake and Tyrolian Lodge way up north, the thing? followed them. Even though he escaped, the bad guys have been looking ever since for whatever he left there when he disappeared."

"So no one ever heard from Johnny again? Is that right?"

"That's right."

"Is there anything else you can tell me about the earrings? Aside from their connection to the Cleary mansion, each victim — Susan Sedgeway and Claudia Reinert — was wearing these very same earrings on the night she was murdered."

Lucas turned toward her and they started to walk back along the lake toward boats and docks.

"They look vaguely familiar," he said, shoving his bony hands stiffly into his pockets.

Glenda eyed him carefully. She always admired a man who couldn't help but wear his feelings on his sleeve. Unlike Miranda and Chick and the odd women from the night of Susan's murder, Lucas was no actor.

"Lucas — someone else may end up murdered! Whoever was after Susan and Claudia obviously knew them, or at least knew who they were. Now, this could be any one of several suspects. It could be Leo himself, Griz, or Monty Simms, the club owner, just to name a few. It might even be a jealous musical rival, like Miranda or Chick."

Lucas nodded as they walked, as if her words only confirmed what he'd thought all along.

"Not to mention Carolyn Stind."

"The professor friend of Griz's? Why?"

He laughed cynically, and Glenda thought how uncharacteristic it sounded. This was not the man she thought she'd perceived just moments ago.

"I have been a collector of various items for decades. But I've never seen a collector like that woman!"

"What does she collect?" Glenda said, although she knew very well.

"Not what — *who*. She's attracted to younger gentlemen. And lately she's had her eye on Tony Manzetti."

"Manzetti? Susan's boyfriend?"

"Susan and Tony were affianced, from what Jake and Pamela told me," Lucas said.

"Interesting. Love or jealousy can be motivating factors. But why Claudia? Why murder her too?"

"Maybe she knew something. You know, for all her scholarship, Professor Stind is money-hungry."

Glenda followed him to the sand-swept parking lot.

"I didn't know Manzetti came from money too." Glenda said.

"No one knows for sure. Manzetti works hard, and his work and family are a private matter to him. But his friends can't say enough good things about him. He was Leo's roommate for a while."

They stood by Glenda's Volvo. She waited, her eyes on Lucas.

"As far as women go, though, Manzetti doesn't know how to treat them," he said sadly.

Glenda thought of Susan and Claudia. "He likes them benign, blonde and buxom, right?"

"You know both the young women who were murdered were involved in that supernatural stuff, you know — Ouija boards and seances and all that. They were roommates in their sorority at University of Illinois."

"Didn't they both date Manzetti too?" Glenda said.

He nodded, then frowned, studying the ground. He seemed afraid of what would come next.

"I'd like to see the cabins," Glenda said firmly. "This Tyrolian Lodge you're talking about in Wisconsin — who or what is the connection up there?"

"It was a haven for my father. In the days of gangsters like Dillinger, and mobsters like Capone, it served as a hideout. I think my son was intrigued by his great-grandfather Siberius' stories. His imagination was piqued by the legends of the mob era. But I'm worried that it went beyond that. I think Siberius told him things in confidence about clandestine visitors up north — about the people and perhaps more."

"You mean what the real racket is now?"

Lucas nodded, his wise old eyes creased and intense.

"I must see Little Tyrolian Lodge, Lucas."

His smile faded and his eyes softened, almost tearful.

"But what will you find now?"

"I think that whatever the scam was seventy years ago is still active today. It had to be more than Prohibition, whores, and the numbers."

"It's a three-hour drive."

"Give me tomorrow. I'll get us there."

Lucas opened the door to his old Mercedes. His hand trembled when he pulled out his keys and fussed about for the ignition. The back seats were laden with boxes full of jewelry, lampshades, bell jars, and vintage clothes.

"We'll take my car," Glenda said simply.

******

They started at dawn. Glenda whipped into a Dunkin' Donuts and ordered a jumbo coffee to go and a box of Munchkins. Seated in the passenger side, Lucas looked as stiff as his starched collar. "Relaxed wear," as Glenda had suggested, was apparently to him a less formal pair of breeches and medium starch. He stared at the box of Munchkins in his lap, like a foreigner in the modern land of fast food.

"They're donuts. Help yourself," she said, backing out of the parking lot.

The first hour of the trip rolled them from city to corn fields to flat prairie land. As they drove further north and it grew colder, Glenda pulled over now and then to pile on sweatshirts and cardigans. Lucas finally accepted one of Jack's oversized Northwestern sweatshirts. Glenda stifled a laugh at the dangling purple sleeves of the sweatshirt, and Lucas' black collar, which stuck up around his neck.

Around twenty minutes from the town of Little Tyrol, Lucas' demeanor changed noticeably. Glenda saw him wringing his hands over and over. Soon they passed through the downtown area, with the usual coffee shops, antique stores and corner groceries. At a stoplight, Glenda noticed a garish looking pawn shop with odds and ends and even some strange musical instruments in the window. At the front of the window display, Glenda spotted several old player piano rolls.

"What's that place?" Glenda said, pointing to the pawn shop. "Looks like there might be some black magic going on."

Lucas cleared his throat and looked down the street in the other direction.

"Where?" he said.

"Right there," she pointed. "Let's go in, can we? Very quickly? I take an interest in these things — antique business and all."

She pulled up and parked. "I'll wait here," Lucas said stubbornly.

"Afternoon," she said, moments later, waltzing into the shop.

"I'm Glenda Dominique from Chicago. Just checking out your place. I own an antique store back home."

He extended his hand to her. "Name's Mack. Good to meet you. Look around all you want."

Glenda noticed an abundance of curious artifacts and macabre devices. She wondered how customers, especially from this rural area, could find anything they would need or want. It struck her that he wanted to keep customers away. Then she spotted a player piano and numerous piano rolls stacked up individually and in boxes marked "Piano rolls." Leaning closer to the boxes she saw a return address which read "Tony Manzetti."

Interesting, she thought. "Thanks Mack," she said, exiting the shop.

She clicked on her seat belt and turned to Lucas. "Which way from here?"

He pointed straight ahead with his long and bony finger toward the end of a cul-de-sac. Just as they arrived, the skies turned grey; the once-full clouds no longer swirled in innocent, imaginative shapes, but rather flatlined in a threatening, pregnant stretch of horizon waiting to burst.

As she drove down the long driveway leading to the cabins, she thought back to the days of Cleary's Club, the speakeasies and Prohibition. What kind of racket did Johnny Cleary and his unscrupulous father Jeremiah have going, she wondered? How did it involve this part of the country? And if they were running from the club, was it from the police or the mob or other thugs? If they were hiding out during certain periods from Cleary's Club, was it from big name Chicago mobsters or just other small time hoods like themselves, who ran similar clubs and small groceries and shops?

"Lucas? What was the Johnny Cleary connection up here in Wisconsin? It was a hideout, but from what?"

"My father, Siberius, helped Johnny and his cohorts allow things to cool down back at the club by coming up here. Then, to keep busy, they got involved up here too. I know it was something illegal, some product they peddled and Siberius MacDougal and Johnny Cleary didn't want big name bosses to know about their operation for fear it would be taken over. At the same time, they didn't want the police to know either of course. So when authorities would get suspicious about dealings at the club, or what the racket was they had going, MacDougal, Cleary and his friends would hide out up here."

As they pulled up to the log cabin nestled in the tall pines, Glenda felt that something was amiss. Lucas coughed as they unloaded the car, then sneezed.

"Get some rest," Glenda said, opening his door. "I'll unload the car and go into town for groceries. I think I saw a Piggly Wiggly on the way in."

"I'm fine," he said gruffly.

If she hadn't known better, she'd have sworn he was afraid. She unpacked her small duffel bag, slung it over her shoulder, and grabbed the cooler of food for the weekend. She walked to the small cabins they were to stay in. Jack would fly up Saturday morning and then drive back with Glenda and Lucas. Returning to the car, she yanked on Lucas' heavy trunk in back. It barely budged. He raced to her.

"Careful! That's an original Louis Vuitton steamship trunk from nineteen-thirty."

"What do you have in here? Bricks?"

He grinned proudly as he took hold of the leather strap on the other side.

"It's my lifeblood. My old books and vintage jewelry. I need to repair and appraise them for an antique shop on Lincoln Avenue near Halsted. I never go anywhere without my work."

As he emerged from the old car, he placed his hands on the small of his long back and stretched. The towering pines, so green they looked black, swayed and bowed in a gusty northerly breeze. The surroundings breathed a mysterious isolation steeped in history and deceit.

They carried Lucas' heavy trunk carefully up the cedar-wood stairs of the cabin and lowered it down by the low stone fireplace.

"I should be back in roughly half an hour. Then we'll examine your father's property. Is it far from here?"

Lucas looked at her and through her at the same time.

"I think it's in walking distance."

"You think?"

Glenda paused by the driver's side of the car and gave him a look where he stood in the shrouded doorway. He looked older all at once.

"Don't you know where it is?" she asked, dubious.

She felt a chilly breeze and looked at the black shadows and the remaining sunlight flickering in and around the lawn. Leaves on the birch trees had changed into golds, reds, and warm browns.

"I knew where it was blindfolded when I was a boy, but that was decades ago. Now I'm not so sure anymore." He stepped back into the cabin, one hand to his head. Glenda felt a pang of guilt for pushing him so hard.

"Look, I'll rustle up some food. Any requests? We're just here through Monday."

"Cigars. Couple of Cubans. I know they carry 'em up here. They have since the Dillinger days."

Glenda nodded and got in the car. With the keys in the ignition, she paused, wondering if she should leave him alone, then shook her head and started up the car.

The pine trees dwarfed her and her Volvo. They looked hundreds of years old. Between them were squeezed delicate but sturdy poplars and more birch trees — some thin as they stretched skywards, others older than any she'd ever seen in Illinois.

Thinking of the Prairie state now, she realized how busy she'd been since moving back to Rosedale with Jack. They'd not taken any time together. The thought of him coming up for even two days unnerved her. They'd grown apart of late, especially since Susan's death.

Sitting at the only stoplight in town, Glenda realized how much her obsession with finding Susan's killer had to do with that emotional distance from Jack. It had often made him angry with her lately. It was clear to Glenda that Jack was jealous of her past with Susan, her "wild years." Somehow Jack saw this whole investigation, and Glenda's intense interest in it as an uncoupling from him and a way for Glenda to relive a time in her life that didn't include him.

She found the corner grocery, and forty minutes later, pulled into the long, now nearly black, driveway of the cabins. A bag of groceries in one arm, she knocked on Lucas' cabin door.

After waiting several minutes, and trying the door, she went to the side and peered in a window. He's definitely not home, she thought, alarmed. Where did he go?

After stashing the groceries in her own cabin, Glenda went in search of him. She knew she had little time to search with the waning daylight.

As she crept through the damp leaves and broken branches, every snap made her jump. She recalled Lucas mentioning that one went due east of the cabin, toward the lake, in order to find the MacDougal property called Tyrolian Lodge. Yet as she continued to walk, she felt the instinctive Morgan defect kick in: Glenda was lost. No one in her family had a sense of direction. She and her mother had managed to navigate through the city of London solely thanks to the kindness of strangers. She grew worried now, because there were no bobbies around to rescue her nor any dimly-lit pubs with their welcome warmth of bad stew and warm bitters. There were only the unrelenting damp and cold, the increasing darkness. And no sound of life, nor of Lucas.

An hour passed. She decided that if necessary, she'd spend the night under a pile of leaves for warmth, even though deep down she knew she couldn't survive that. The temperature had dropped to around forty degrees and the forest looked as black as a blanket of death. Taking a deep breath, she had crouched to gather what branches and leaves she could for cover when suddenly a tiny light filtered through the trees. She smelled smoke and saw a pulse of life: a fireplace.

She got up and staggered toward the light and the comforting scent of childhood camp-outs. Soon she came upon an old cabin. Around the windows were thick shutters; a massive porch ran the length of the front. The slanted wooden roof reminded her of the finer Stickley style bungalows seen in California. A lot of money here, she thought, her heart racing. Ill-gotten? Mob?

Then she saw Lucas. He sat by a Tiffany lamp that shone through lace curtains. Behind him, she could make out flickering flames from a generous fireplace.

"Damn it, Lucas," she said, knocking on the door.

She waited and after a moment, she heard sounds of shuffling and coughing. Finally the heavy door swung open. The air from outside wafted into the room, combining with the smells of dust and aged knotty pine.

"You deserted me, Lucas! I have no sense of direction!"

He paced around the room, his eyes on Glenda, which was unusual for him. "I wasn't sure I'd find it myself. I feel disloyal allowing you in here."

"Disloyal to whom? I know it's a cover for something else. What is it you don't want me to know about?"

As if struck, he threw himself into a chair, his face in his hands. Rubbing his forehead, he mumbled, "That's just it, I don't know what there is to hide. He never told me."

"Who didn't?"

All at once Glenda's heart went out to him. She walked over to the chair, laid her hand on his shoulder and knelt down. The fire felt warm.

"My father," said Lucas. "Siberius was closer to Jake. He trusted him. But little Jake didn't understand the gravity of what he was told; he thought it was all cops and robbers. It's much more sinister. Siberius had formed the Six Dixies when the club opened in the nineteen-twenties. He would have done anything to help his friend Johnny Cleary and keep the club going — *Anything*, even if it meant innocent people died or went to jail. And there's still a racket going on — I just don't know what it is."

He sounded on the verge of tears. Glenda settled on a duck-patterned ottoman in front of him. As she looked around the room, she noticed silver candlesticks and cherrywood antiques everywhere.

"You have to understand that two innocent women have died because of whatever it is you're not telling me," she said.

"It's here. I know the goods are here. I don't know what or where, though. I swear to you."

"Do you mind if I look around? I've narrowed down the connection to this place. You're the vintage jewelry expert. What do you think?"

"You mean the earrings?"

"You have to admit, both murdered women having worn them is pretty strange. What — or who — do you think is the connection?"

He was silent.

"Okay," she said. "I think it could be Griz, or even Professor Stind. They could be in it together. But what would the motive be? Money? Griz could be in on it with Cleary. They're friends, right? Maybe since booze is no longer lucrative, they've moved into drugs. Or what about the two people profiled on the earrings? All we know is that they represent the two statues situated out in front of the old mansion. So that connects the Clearys, at least the old Cleary family, to the jewelry. But what is it we're missing about this place?" she said, walking around the room.

Lucas rose, as if to evade her question, and placed a pot of water on the stove. "Wonder if this old thing still works?" he said, leaning over. "I'll light the pilot and make us some tea. I used to come here as a child. The place still haunts me. I guess it's because I never understood what really went on in this strange beautiful place — this untouched pearl in Wisconsin."

Examining the two bedrooms, Glenda felt along the pine walls searching for anything — a hidden door, a closet unopened for decades. After a while, she grew dismayed as she reached the small dining room with cherrywood trim all around the ceiling and baseboards. She felt along a built-in hutch in the corner and a sideboard filled with gold and white china. As she returned to the living room where the fire crackled, she noticed an upright piano behind the door in the foyer that she'd missed seeing when she first came in. It resembled the one at Cleary's Club.

"Well, here's something interesting," remarked Glenda.

"What?"

"You'd think that with all the musical talent that used to hide out up here they'd have the piano in a more prominent place, don't you?"

He followed her to the foyer with brimming cups of tea.

"Isn't this strange?" asked Glenda, turning to look at him over her shoulder as she lifted the lid up over the ivory piano keys.

Sliding onto an ink-black seat embroidered in ornate red and gold needlepoint, she began to play a Chopin piece. But instead of the usual forthright sounds of a well-tuned piano, the keys made only thudding sounds, as if no pads existed inside the mechanism to make contact with strings or pedals.

"What on earth?" exclaimed Glenda, attempting to lift open the black sliding door above the keys. "It's locked! I've never heard of such a thing."

"Oh, my Lord," said Lucas, setting the teacups down on a nearby table. "We'd better leave it alone."

"Hand me that knife over there," she said, indicating a steak knife he'd used to cut back the wax of a candle.

"I don't know if we should. What if they find out?"

"Who?" demanded Glenda, her tone firm.

He hesitated. "Cleary's has been doing so well lately. And Griz is involved. That's why he beat up poor Pamela. I can't put her in any more danger!"

"Lucas. People have died," she said evenly. "Give me the knife."

Prying at the aged gold lock, Glenda scraped back some rotten wood, then shoved the knife into the side of the instrument.

"I'm sorry, old thing," she said, patting the piano, "but I have to see your guts!"

As she said this, the piano's lock cracked open. Inside the space where there would normally be strings were hundreds of rolls, like those used for a player piano.

"It's just a bunch of piano rolls," Lucas said, relieved, falling back on the nearby sofa. "Thank God."

But Glenda didn't speak. Grabbing one of the rolls, she dug around inside. "The entire piano is empty; it's just a container for these rolls. There are no working parts inside."

With this she pulled out more rolls and began tearing at one. As she did so its contents spilled out. She knelt down and retrieved several pairs of earrings identical to those worn by Susan Sedgeway and Claudia Reinert. The two sculpted profiles on the cameos depicted the statues outside the Cleary family's Pinehurst mansion.

"And here's the key to the entire puzzle! This is no ordinary piano, Lucas."

She turned to face him but he merely stared, his mouth open.

Chapter Fifteen

Jack arrived the next morning and all three decided to drive back to Chicago immediately.

"Glenda! Slow down!" Lucas screamed.

"Not to worry, Lucas. She's a good driver," Jack said. "But I don't get what the hurry is."

Glenda pounded the wheel at the stoplight waiting for the green. It was the only stoplight in town. "I'm certain Pamela Burke is in danger," she said.

Lucas slid forward from the back seat to look at her.

"I've been worried all along, especially about Griz's connection to her. Why are you worried about Pamela?"

"I'm sorry, Lucas. I know you're already concerned. Just tell me, is there someone we can call?"

"We can try Jake."

"Use my car phone," she said, handing it to him. "Hit nine first."

"But why Pamela?" he repeated, dialing the number.

"When I came to your house yesterday," Glenda said, "she told me I should ask Griz about the mob connections to Cleary's. Granted, I know she let that slip by mistake, but if that's just a small taste of what she knows, I think she's in trouble."

"Thank God," Lucas said, holding the phone. "It's ringing."

Glenda honked at a car going twenty miles an hour, the driver pointing to houses to his passenger as they went along.

"Come on, Sunday driver!"

She whipped around him. Lucas held on awkwardly by pressing his hand upward to the roof of the car.

"No answer," he said, his voice tight.

"We'll be home soon," Glenda said, patting his shoulder. "I'll make sure of it."

Jack leaned over and touched her arm.

"Glen, about the other night? Our talk about Griz and your drinking?"

She glanced at him, then back at the road.

"I'm sorry," he said.

"I know," she replied. "It's okay."

Jack sat back. "What's the plan once we get there?" he said. "I'm sure you have something up your sleeve and as usual, I'd better gauge how outrageous it is."

"Well," Glenda said, smiling, "we're going to try to reach Pamela for the next hour or so. Once home, I think we should go directly to the Cleary mansion in Pinehurst, the one with the statues out front that match the earrings."

"Why?" Lucas said. "Young Leo doesn't live there."

"I know," Glenda said, slyly. "From what I heard, he lives in some trendy converted loft when he's in the city — plus he has that monstrous house in North Kenwood where Claudia was murdered. But it's not him I'm interested in. I want to know what's going on at the house in Pinehurst."

"How is it significant?" Jack said, studying a road map.

"The earrings, for one thing. And the fact that the house has been in the Cleary family for generations. First of all, that connects the Clearys through the earrings and statues, to the murders of Susan and Claudia."

Jack looked skeptical. Glenda could see his hesitation and it raised her Scottish ire.

"What?" she said, glaring at him fiercely.

"I think you're going overboard because Susan was your friend. How do we know the two murders are connected? And how do we know there's only one murderer?"

"I don't know anything, Jack. It's an educated guess. I think the two women are involved in the racket because the earrings connect them. The earrings were limited-edition forgeries. I've checked with all the big-name retailers and jewelers in Chicago, New York and Los Angeles and none have heard of the company listed on the back of the earrings that are held in evidence with Detective Halloran at the North Kenwood police station."

"You talked to him?"

"I called him to see if there was anything written on the back of them, and he said no. But when a buddy of mine at the station, Officer Schmidt, read them again for me under a microscope, they read simply "LT" — which I think stands for Little Tyrol. So I realized they weren't intended as mainstream costume jewelry. They were forgeries. I also discovered from my own research from connections in the business and owning the antique store myself that there *is* an original pair of earrings like the ones Susan and Claudia wore — but only one. They were commissioned by Johnny Cleary for Rose Green."

"Why on earth were the women wearing them out in public then?" asked Lucas.

"That's the point. I don't think they were supposed to be. Either they just didn't know or — as I think is the case with Claudia — they were trying to upset or tip off someone."

"You said you thought that was the case with Claudia, right Glen?" Jack said. "But you'd only seen her that night at Cleary's party in North Kenwood."

"But I watched her. I noticed how she kept fingering the earrings that night of the party. She was definitely sending a message to someone."

"How do you know that?" asked Jack skeptically.

"Because I know women."

As she spoke, she slowed down to the toll booth, paid the toll, and raced onwards.

"Look," she said, "I'm taking the exit to Pinehurst. We're going to the Cleary mansion."

"No one lives there any more," said Lucas dubiously.

Jack nodded. "I've heard the place is barely maintained by monthly groundskeepers. We won't find anyone there."

"We *will* find something," said Glenda determinedly. "I just have a feeling."

Soon after, she pulled over to the side of a quiet residential street.

"My God," Lucas said. "We're here. I had no idea we'd reached Pinehurst already."

"Be careful," Jack put in. "I've heard the cops around here are always itching to pick someone up for speeding or loitering."

"Here's the plan," Glenda said. "Should we find anyone on the premises, one of us should do the scouting while the other two pretend they're looking for another address."

"Let me guess who the scout's gonna be," smirked Jack.

"I think I'm best qualified," Glenda agreed amicably.

Witnesses while we're at it?" asked Jack. "We don't have a name or a reason for being here."

Glenda started to drive up the street. "Look, this is Elm Street. Poplar Street is the next one over. That's where the Cleary house is. Tell whomever answers that you're looking for that house," she said, pointing to an enormous brown Tudor house where two red-haired dogs sat regally on the lawn. "Say you'd heard there was a breeder of Irish setters around here. You just can't remember the name they gave, but they lived on the twelve-hundred block of Elm or Poplar. That's close enough to knowing someone in the neighborhood."

"Seems flimsy," Lucas said, looking doubtful. "They might know my house in Rosedale. And my picture's been in the paper a lot. I think maybe Jack should go up alone. I'll man the wheel."

Glenda smiled. "We need someone to look for people, photographs — any connections to anyone outside the Cleary family, like old-timer bosses. That's why I think you're going to have to go in, Lucas. You know more of the history of the town and Chicago. No offense, Jack. Lucas, you'll recognize people he won't. That's what we're looking for."

"Let's try Pamela one more time," Lucas said.

He dialed the number, then nodded excitedly.

"Hello, Jake? Where's Pamela?" The color drained from Lucas' face. "What do you mean? When was that?" He put down the car phone.

"She said she was lying down to rest, but when he checked on her, she was gone. He has no idea where she is."

His voice trembled. Glenda patted his hand.

"We'll find her, Lucas. Let's see what we can uncover here first."

Although they'd made good time from Wisconsin, the sky had already clouded and turned charcoal grey. Glenda crept alongside the mansion, through the bushes, then darted into the backyard. She ran past a gazebo with a white trellis peppered with tiny purple flowers. Suddenly she spotted movement in the ground floor of the house. Peering from behind a large oak tree, she gazed into a study filled with rows of leather-bound books. Oddly, there didn't seem to be any lights on. Flashlights played quickly back and forth, however, and Glenda watched the lights as they swept from the study down a hallway and into rooms at the other end of the house.

Then she simultaneously heard the chime of doorbells and the splashing sounds of water. A pool, she thought?Crouching as much as she could behind bushes, she crept nearer to the sounds of water and spied a large kidney-shaped swimming pool. Glenda recognized

Chick Natale, voluptuous in a sleek one-piece bathing suit, as she left the pool and wrapped a towel around her tiny waist. An autumn swim, Glenda thought. Chick must like the cold. As Chick neared the back door, the flickering lights inside the house vanished. Kneeling, Chick took a key from under the mat and let herself in through the back door to the kitchen.

Closing in on the house, Glenda noticed that a door apparently leading down to a basement had been left ajar. Without hesitating she ran down the flight of stairs and slipped inside the house. As she wiped away clinging cobwebs, she smelled the unmistakable scent described by Jeremy, the young DePaul music student: "That bath stuff, like scented candles." My God, she thought, remembering the nightclub haunting, it's the lavender. Instinctively she backed up against the wall. As she did so, her shoes scraped against something gritty.

These are new Reeboks, she thought. They can't have that much debris under them already. Am I losing my mind? It's being in the Cleary mansion that's pushing me off the deep end.

Then a flash of white collar and a dark-clad form rushed past, fleeing down some sort of stone corridor. Determined, Glenda followed, feeling her way along the wall.

After five minutes in the darkness, with the ever-present scent of lavender and violets swirling about her in the room, she saw a faint light spilling down the steep flight of cellar stairs. Then she heard voices from upstairs.

"I really don't know what I can do for you, Mr. Dougal," a woman said, her voice shrill.

"*Mac*Dougal. Well, Ms. Natale, we met some time ago. It may have been at the University, perhaps in music school. I've lectured at Northwestern and DePaul Universities."

"Whatever. I'm not authorized to let just anyone in here."

Lucas' heavy boots clomped from one room to another as he moved across the hardwood floors of what had to be the hall and upstairs rooms. Good for you, old boy, Glenda thought. Keep it up.

Soon Chick stomped onto the back deck with Lucas in tow. Why had she brought him outside, Glenda wondered? Was she hiding something?

"For God's sake let me find a wrap," she snapped, sounding strained. "All right, I'll answer a few questions. But then you'll have to go. I have to be somewhere."

"Thank you, miss. I'm sure you're busy," Lucas said, stalling. "Now you were a music student at DePaul, is that right?"

"I finished my training there. I started out at University of Illinois music school in Champaign. That's where I met Cleary and Tony Manzetti. Cleary transferred the same time I did, and then did graduate school at DePaul too. Why?"

"I just need to know how well you know Professor Gordon Glenn. He's also friends with Tony Manzetti and Leo Cleary. My friends and I think there is some connection between the racket going on out of Wisconsin and Griz and the mob. Come now, Ms. Natale."

"What racket? Why would I know about some illegal operation?"

"I didn't say 'illegal.' Why did you?"

Glenda sensed mounting tension. She climbed the rest of the stairs quickly. Glancing into the room, she was awestruck by the elegance before her. Vaulted ceilings, mahogany antiques, and an elegant, spacious parlor were visible to the left. Although dusty, the salon spilled over with red velvet — chairs, divans, and ottomans, doubtless for the porcelain-skinned ladies of the house at the turn of the century to retire over tea and conversation. In the center of the room was a marble table, surrounded by fake ferns and hanging plants. But the most spectacular feature was a richly-colored tapestry draped over the entranceway. Glenda gazed at it for a long minute, trying to remember where she'd seen it before.

"I think you'd better leave," Chick said. "Now."

Glenda stepped into the room just as Lucas rose from an ornate sofa.

"Lucas — wait," Glenda said, stalking across the glossy hardwood floor until she stood directly in front of Chick. The startled actress yanked a flimsy periwinkle-blue robe more tightly around her shoulders. "If you won't talk to him," she said, evenly, "talk to me."

"How the hell did you get in here? I'm calling the police," said Chick, slinking toward an old-fashioned white telephone.

"You seem nervous, Chick. What — or who — are you hiding?"

"Why don't you ask Pamela Burke? I thought she was your star witness."

Glenda didn't flinch. "She claims she saw nothing. The police have thoroughly questioned both Cleary and Pamela. All she said was that Manzetti had gone to get her a drink, *not* a drink for Susan."

Glenda paced the circumference of the room as she spoke. Chick, in her turn, paced a small patch of the Oriental rug, her eye makeup looking as heavy as if she'd come from a nightclub instead of the pool. Glenda glanced around the old-fashioned living room, trying to spot photographs, artifacts, or any connection to the history of Cleary's Club or the mob. She noticed a time-gone-by feel about the place, as if it had been preserved but not updated. Chick had backed up against a white mantel, behind a simple green deco-style sofa.

"I think you'd both better leave," she said, crossing her arms over her chest.

"Why are you here?" Glenda asked, studying her intently.

"Leo lets me use the place whenever I want. We're friends." She scrutinized Glenda. "*Good* friends."

"That may be true," Lucas commented. "But I know this timeless house has not been used in years. It's maintained, that's all."

"Shows what you don't know!"

"Tell us about Griz," Glenda urged. "We've run out of time. Tell us — or we'll go to him. I want to know about the forgeries and the jewelry racket."

"Look," said Chick, her voice uneven, "Susan and Claudia were fools. The women believed Griz when he promised money and fame as models. You should know. Susan was an opportunist. She'd have done anything to break into the elite circles. She tried to be something she wasn't. She was a cheap, gold-digging social climber. She died of an overdose. It's over."

Glenda endured this tirade in silence. She watched the nervous tics as the statuesque and lovely, yet troubled, actress before her unfold. As Chick spoke, she fluffed her thick brown bobbed hair, and her green catlike eyes flashed.

"I don't care about your opinion of Susan," Glenda said. "Lucas and I have been to Wisconsin. We know about the forgeries — and we know Griz is involved."

"Look," Chick said, her voice trembling suddenly. "All I know is, Susan and Claudia were the transportation part of the operation. They wined and dined the big timers, the dealers. You know what an expert Susan was at overindulgence and Tony was damn sick of it. Tony's a mover. He was sick of her behavior, I know that."

"Is that why Carolyn Stind was moving in for the kill?" Glenda said.

Lucas gasped as if he thought Glenda had gone too far. He'd been leaning against a mahogany rolltop desk and now knocked several papers off, sending them to the floor. Chick noticed him and stalked over.

"I want both of you out," she said, retrieving the papers. "Now! It's the last time I'll ask."

Glenda and Lucas headed for the door, but then Glenda turned around abruptly. "Why is the Cleary Club ghost at the house? I know what a tight-knit, theatrical group you are. Who's the performer?"

"There's no one else here," Chick said. "I'm alone. I have a key, like I said."

"We're going," murmured Glenda, heeding Lucas' look of panic.

******

"Lucas — We've got to find Pamela! Money-hungry people are involved here."

"What about Jack?"

"We'll come back for him," Glenda said.

As they reached the next block, on the horizon, the moon looked bold and menacing. Glenda stamped on the brakes when a dark-haired, unshaven man wandered out in front of the car. His hair was slicked back, his white collar stiff. He wore black tails and shiny black shoes.

"My God, it's Leo Cleary!" cried Glenda. "Lucas, jump out. See if he's okay."

Getting laboriously out of the passenger seat, Lucas shuffled over and extended his arms to the young musician. But Leo seemed strangely oblivious to them. Glenda waited in the car, glancing in the rear-view mirror. Seconds later she spotted Chick Natale at the wheel of her Porsche 911, with Griz in the passenger seat of the car. They were arguing heatedly. Then Chick's eyes met Glenda's and with a screech of the wheels, she whipped her car around them, flooring it through a red light and missing Leo and Lucas by inches.

Throwing open the back door, Lucas pushed Leo gently into the back seat and sat down himself in the passenger seat. Lucas looked drained.

"What's wrong with Leo?" he asked.

Glenda shook her head. "Aside from alcohol, I suspect he's been into drugs too, for a while."

Glenda pulled up to a diner. Although the facade looked like a typical 1950s American diner, it sported the usual Pinehurst excesses: a brick-and-ivy outdoor cafe with Cinzano umbrellas and lace curtains billowing from the windows.

"Let's get him some coffee. He has a performance tonight. And he may know where Pamela is. Isn't that right, Leo?"

Leo looked up, his eyes boring through Glenda's in the rear-view mirror.

"My name is Johnny, Johnny Cleary. You're a singer at the club, aren't you, dear?" he said dreamily.

Glenda parked, climbed out of the car, and rushed to the back. Lucas had opened the door.

"Is he drunk?" asked Lucas.

"Probably. Come on, Johnny. We need to talk about the club."

"The club, the club," he muttered as they piled into a corner booth. "I've done all I can."

"Talk to us," Glenda said, flagging a waitress and indicating their empty coffee cups.

"I've done all I can. I've played the music. I've brought the old days alive, man! Rose Green and Doc Reilly....They were in love. But I didn't kill them. Griz is overboard, he's like Reilly. I tried to please father by bringing in money. Griz had the ideas – the girls would take care of the dealers. That was all!"

Lucas looked baffled. Glenda shook her head, finger to her mouth. Several well-starched patrons frowned upon the scene.

"Leo, concentrate. Are you performing at the club later on tonight?"

"I'm the opening act and the closing. I'm it. But the club's going under anyway. And Manzetti..."

"What about Manzetti?" asked Glenda.

"He's playing something tonight too."

Lucas sighed. "He's missing the point, isn't he?" he whispered.

Glenda called the waitress again.

"How about a plate of spaghetti for our friend?" she asked. Then she turned to Lucas. "Let's fill him up with some carbohydrates."

Leo turned to her, his eyes now lucid.

"I'm all right, actually. Reality is creeping in as the wine wears off. I'm going to lose the club — in more ways than one. After all I've done! I never should have let Griz talk me into all the crazy shit."

Glenda nodded, stifling a grin. Although his brain was somewhat fried from drugs, she thought Leo Cleary had definite charm. He'd started to grow a beard again. And in that moment, she realized why she'd never suspected Cleary of playing ghost on the night of Susan's murder: the beard. He couldn't possibly have had time to shave the night of Susan's murder.

"Johnny didn't visit the night of Susan's murder, did he?" Glenda said, simply. "He didn't make a guest appearance at the club?"

Leo eyed her carefully, his blue eyes narrowed.

"That wasn't me. Heard about it, though. Whoever it was knows his music. According to Monty, it sounded like me."

"So you really had left the club like you told the police?" Glenda said.

"You bet."

"Then tell me," she said, "who else knows the 'Maple Leaf Rag' and the Johnny Cleary routine as well as you do?"

Leo smiled — an exceedingly sexy smile. "That would have to be my old roommate."

"Tony Manzetti?" Glenda said.

"He's the master imitator."

Glenda rubbed her forehead, deep in thought. She noticed the troubled look on Lucas' face and followed his gaze, through the fork-and-spoon clatter and too many ferns, to a corner booth. Seated side by side were Griz and Chick. Across from them, Glenda recognized the back of a familiar blonde head.

Chapter Sixteen

The club was electric tonight. Rumors about the resurgence of the specter of Johnny Cleary had spread throughout the Lincoln Avenue/Halsted/DePaul University area. Tonight's star attraction, Leo Cleary, had spent the early evening with Glenda and Lucas, devouring a plate of spaghetti and drinking an entire pot of coffee.

Now the three, joined by Jack, listened to the continuation of Leo Cleary's tale of woe as they sat before the infamous Cleary Club stage. It was still early and the place was empty. An imposing bouncer had forbidden entry to a long line of grunge-style wannabe's on the street. Leo had let his three companions in through the back door.

As Glenda listened, Monty Simms whipped past their table, followed closely by Griz, who carried a heavy garment over his shoulder. As he brushed past Glenda she spotted two tuxedo tails nearly dragging on the floor. Monty waved at Leo briefly and kept walking.

Glenda asked Lucas for a dollar to buy a Coke; she was running on empty and needed caffeine. As he reached into his wallet, Glenda glimpsed the face of Helen, the disappearing Northwestern librarian, on a snapshot in its plastic photo pages. Glenda quickly changed the subject.

"Lucas, did Rose Green have any friends in the Six Dixies that you recall? Even very young friends?"

He looked away furtively. Then he spotted the photo in his wallet and he snatched it back quickly.

"No."

"Not even someone who would be quite elderly today? Someone close to the music scene, someone who may work in the industry? Or perhaps in a library?"

Leo looked foggy as he eyed Glenda, then Lucas.

"The ironic thing is, Lucas, I met someone — a librarian at the music library at Northwestern — who strongly resembled you. She is your sister, isn't she, Lucas? Why are you protecting her?"

Lucas bowed his head. Leo's mouth was agape.

"Your sister?" he said. "I thought she died."

Lucas looked up finally. "Helen's alive and yes, she's a librarian at the music library. They thought she was crazy at first...but then the police wouldn't leave her alone. She knew that the murders of Doc Reilly and Rose Green had less to do with love than with greed. I suspect they were hits, pure and simple. Helen was a witness.... She was married at seventeen. That's why her name was Moss. He died in the war."

Leo shook his head. "But I've been looking for the lady for years! She could have proved my grandfather's innocence! I'd heard she'd died — everyone thought so."

"That's the way she wanted it, right Lucas?" Glenda put in. "For her own protection?"

He nodded.

"And that's why she disappeared the afternoon I was nosing around the library searching for the Six Dixies files."

"She thought you'd recognize her. She even tried to scare you off by creating — a supernatural incident, I guess you'd call it. The guard didn't know she was there. It was her morning off. She went in to catch up on paperwork."

"You know, Leo," Glenda said, turning to the handsome musician, "I've been haunted by a statement quoted in a *Vanity Fair* from the nineteen-twenties that I stumbled on at my store. It was made by your great grandfather. He said that before he'd rest in peace in death, he would come back to set the record straight. Now I think that was all theatrics on his part; that kind of flamboyant nature runs in your family. He wanted the right people to think he was dead. But you knew about that threat and you've been using it to revive the ghost thing, haven't you?"

Leo smiled. His blue eyes danced mischievously.

"You got me," he said. "People expect it. The act, I mean. They've heard about it for years, but I make the appearances elusive enough to excite interest. You know the score."

"And that's why you played that cat-and-mouse game with me in the practice rooms at DePaul University. *You* were the specter in theatrical makeup! You know I'd follow you."

He nodded sullenly. Then his face changed. "But believe me, I don't know how the murderer got away with killing Susan. I mean, I'd already left, so I have an alibi. But if someone slipped her something, even as obviously as putting it in her drink, wouldn't it have been spotted?"

"Detective O'Hara, he's on the case," Glenda said. "He said he questioned everyone, even Pamela Burke. Chick Natale mentioned that Susan was late joining the rest of us in the party the night at the club because she was visiting you backstage."

"That's right," Leo said with a smirk. "Seems to be the habit of many of my girlfriends."

Lucas turned on him. "What the sam hill's that supposed to mean, you damn womanizer?"

Glenda touched Lucas' arm.

"What was the routine?" she asked.

"The women I became romantically involved with used to hang around the club backstage while I warmed up, you know, tested out the reeds and tuned up. Susan particularly liked playing my soprano sax now and then. She found it sexy and exciting, the whole musician mystique, you know. But that night I got mad at her."

"Why?" Glenda said.

"She messed up my reeds, man. I had them soaking in a glass of water like I always do and she was sucking on them, you know, like they were cigarettes. She was really drunk that night."

"Why was she flirting with you, anyway?" demanded Glenda. "She and Tony had been together for six months."

Leo's blue eyes were intense suddenly. "Women always come back to me, or try to."

Lucas shook his head in disgust. The room was filling up as divas in black filtered in. "Sorry about leading you on, Glenda," Leo said, "the practice-room thing and all. I just thought if I spooked you enough, you'd give up your ghost hunting."

"What didn't you want me to figure out?" Glenda asked. "About the business scheme with Griz? I've seen him at the costume shop. He's been providing the tuxedos for the Johnny Cleary show and you've been the star. And from what I've learned from my New Age friends, the lavender incense and granules are easy to obtain. The simple pressure of the waiter's feet crushes the granules and activates the scents. But the counterfeit racket was more than you bargained for, right? So you agreed to let them use the MacDougal cabin to hide the goods."

"Now that was *not* my doing!" he shouted. "The mob connected with Manzetti's family started that back in the nineteen-thirties. The Cleary and MacDougal families were tight. Johnny Cleary made a deal with the devil back in the twenties to keep his club from going under."

"So you decided to re-establish that deal in the nineties with Griz and Manzetti?"

"I was going to lose the club for good! I had to do *something*! Even my ghost act wasn't bringing in enough business. So I agreed to pull in some of my old music and acting-class buddies, like Chick and Miranda..."

"And Susan and Claudia?" Glenda said.

"Yes. But I didn't kill them! I loved those girls."

"Leo. That was actually the one night you couldn't come up with a bona-fide alibi. You say you'd already left, but nobody really knows that. You didn't do the Johnny Cleary ghost act that night."

"Are you accusing me? If you don't believe my alibi, talk to the damn police. They'll tell you my story."

"This is not necessarily an accusation. But you have to admit, the murderer must have known you wouldn't have your theatrical alibi to fall back on. Maybe he or she was trying to set you up. Now, what duties did your actress friends have to perform?"

Leo sighed, exasperated. "They were just escorts, you know — plus whatever else they were willing or drugged-out enough to do. And they spread the counterfeit jewelry."

"But the mistake was when Susan wore the earrings. They were one-of-a-kind replicas of the Cleary mansion statues."

"I didn't give them to her!"

"Well, someone did. And they obviously had special meaning because the killer also gave Claudia a pair. But actually I have a feeling that Claudia was not *given* her pair. Leo, I noticed on the night of your party how she fingered them and kept staring at you. But what if it wasn't you she was staring at? In other words, simply wearing those earrings may have been a statement. She hoped someone who knew jewelry would catch on that the pair Susan wore the night she died were fakes — or perhaps even the original pair commissioned back in the twenties for the Cleary family."

"But who was she trying to finger?" Lucas said.

"Well, it might be much simpler even than a connection to the forgeries. She may simply have been letting the killer know that she knew who he was. We already know that she'd have had the earrings because she was part of the jewelry-forgery racket. I figure they were smuggled in and out of Little Tyrol via that piano-roll store, under the guise of some sort of antique parts supplier for the player pianos. Who'd even think to look? I know from being in the antique business that once you find a good supplier of piano rolls, you stick with them. And since it was the MacDougal cabin and they were circulated out of Little Tyrol..."

Lucas looked alarmed. "Not Jake? You think he let them use the place?"

"How else would they have gotten access?" Glenda pointed out.

Lucas shook his head, then gulped the remainder of his red wine. "Wouldn't this Claudia have been foolish," he wondered, "to taunt the killer that way?"

Leo laughed. "But that was Claudia, all right! She loved living on the edge. Why else would she have dated Griz, then me — and Manzetti at the same time?"

"She knew Griz intimately?" asked Glenda.

"And Manzetti really well. Look, I have a set to play," said Cleary, rising.

"You really think the Cleary act was bringing in business?"

Leo practically sneered. "Listen to that crowd!" he said. Outside could be heard stomping feet, drunken yells and occasional outbursts of uproarious laughter. "Tell me again how bringing the legend of Johnny Cleary to life hasn't jump-started business!" he said.

"Sure it has — but Griz got you in over your head, didn't he?" countered Glenda.

"Griz does whatever Manzetti tells him to. Anything! Look, they're setting up. I gotta go."

Soon Jack joined Glenda and Lucas and the three sat down. Lucas and Glenda had coffee, while Jack ordered a Budweiser.

"Thanks for deserting me, guys. I took a cab over here."

"The earrings..." Glenda muttered.

"What now?" Jack said.

I had a thought yesterday when I was doing inventory at my antique shop: what if we're dealing with some sort of obsessive-compulsive murderer? Someone who plans each murder, then assigns the victim by giving her a gift just before he murders her?"

"Gift?" wondered Lucas.

"Such as antique earrings. Maybe this whole counterfeit ring has nothing to do with the chain of murders!"

"Like a serial killer?" Jack said. "That could be. I read once that there's usually a pattern of some sort. Ted Bundy, the attorney, liked sorority girls. Maybe you're on to something."

"And maybe this guy — because I think, judging from the strength needed for the second murder by strangulation, that the killer is male — has a thing for actresses. Something definitely connects Susan and Claudia beyond their both being 'escorts' in the jewelry scam. They were also friends in their college sorority."

The place was now filled to capacity. Suddenly Glenda spotted a woman wearing obviously antique earrings made of two distinctive black-and-white cameos. The center bulbs sparkled and looked like preternatural black crystals. Glenda had studied the Polaroid photo well enough to know them a mile away — not to mention the woman's familiar blonde hair and black skirt slit high up one side. She wore her blonde locks up and in loose curls on this night. It was Pamela Burke.

Glenda excused herself and wove in and around small cocktail tables crammed with uproarious revelers. She had to dodge drink-swilling artistic types at every turn, all dressed in black, some with eye-catching accessories like purple scarves, patent-leather shoes, lacy blouses, or red leather. Her mind drifted back to the night of Susan's murder. It all seemed the same now, like a repeat performance. There was something equally eerie about this night, especially the presence of Pamela wearing that same black skirt. It was as if the whole room were a stage set. Finally, Glenda reached the blonde.

"Pamela? Funny seeing you here! And where did you get those earrings?"

When Pamela finally turned her eyes looked furtive, like a wild animal captured suddenly.

"What's it to you?" Glenda hardly recognized Pamela's voice.

"I saw you talking to Chick and Griz at the diner in Pinehurst. I don't know how you're involved, but you're in danger now — you know too much. And the killer has targeted a small circle of actresses involved somehow with Griz and the jewelry ring. Remember that both Susan and Claudia were wearing the same cameo earrings when they were killed."

Pamela grimaced. "You're crazy. Besides, we've practically worked out all the details with Monty Simms. He's going to sell his portion of the club to us and that crazy Cleary will be out of the picture for good."

As Pamela spoke, Glenda noticed a commotion nearby and saw Miranda and Chick running into the ladies' room. But when she turned around again, Pamela had disappeared.

Glenda rushed into the bathroom, and found Miranda Gloucester, wearing red and black sequins and Chick Natale in a fuchsia spandex number, battling it out. Suddenly Chick shoved Miranda, who was inches shorter, into a row of mirrors.

"What's your problem?" Chick said harshly. "You really think Leo is interested in you? You're pathetic! He and I have been working on a play together. Why, I spent the day at his grandparents' pool. I have a key. He lets me come and go as I please — as long as I please him."

Miranda squirmed away, her wide-set dark eyes hard and angry. "You have Griz, you selfish bitch! God knows you'll go to any length for notoriety, even whoring yourself for his and Manzetti's operation. Manzetti's just out to ruin Leo."

Chick laughed cruelly. "Manzetti's latest toy is doing all the work for him. Just like Susan and Claudia — that is, until Susan smartened up and realized, even in her drunken stupor, that Manzetti was nothing more than her pimp. He baited her to do whatever it took to nail down a deal with the jewelry moguls. Manzetti's ruthless."

"He has Griz right where he wants him," Miranda whispered harshly.

At that moment, Glenda recognized Miranda as the woman who'd been with Griz the afternoon he'd turned up at her shop, In Retrospect — when she'd dropped a heavy Shakespeare volume from the second-floor gallery to distract Griz in his abusive fury.

"And," Miranda continued, "your precious Griz introduced Carolyn Stind, the man-crazy professor, to Manzetti. He's been carrying on with her for over a year. That poor sucker Susan was in way over her head."

"Just more of Leo's cast-offs," Chick hissed. "Claudia Reinert was *twice* the fool — first Leo, then Griz!"

"Look, Chick," Miranda said, firmly. "All I know is that you'd better tell Griz to lay off Pamela. Manzetti likes her — but only in his sick obsessive way. Just like he used to keep an eye on Susan like a damn cop. I was there the night she was flirting with Leo backstage

— the same night she was murdered. You should have seen the way he looked at her when he caught her playing around with Leo's soprano saxophone before Leo's set."

"Susan got what she deserved," Chick said, "angering Manzetti that way. And Leo just goes through women like water; he doesn't think twice about them. Now Manzetti, he's a bit more intense..."

Glenda backed up against the wall in the shadows, palms flat, her heart pounding. Griz and Claudia, she thought? Then why did he beat up Pamela at the party? Did she know something? Is Griz the murderer after all?

"Look," Miranda said, "too may women have suffered at the hands of Griz and even Leo Cleary, not to mention those that have died."

Glenda's eyes widened. She held her breath.

"Are you saying you suspect Griz or Leo could have murdered Susan and Claudia?" Chick demanded in disbelief.

"I just don't know. But let's drop the topic of Leo for now," Miranda said, lowering her voice. "I have to get back."

"Fine."

Glenda slipped out of the bathroom quickly. Women are fools, she thought. If she had it all straight, then Susan, Claudia, and Chick were most involved in the jewelry scheme. Also, both Susan and Claudia had been involved first with Leo and then with Manzetti. And somehow Griz knew them all too, at least in a business sense.

Glenda stood back by a side bar, watching Jack and Lucas sitting in silence at a small cocktail table. Lucas looked out of place in this hip, cosmopolitan nightclub, like a district court judge at a rock concert. He sat up straight, his legs crossed stiffly.

Glenda's mind raced. Both murdered women had been found wearing the earrings; the first was somehow poisoned, the second strangled. Glenda realized now that she probably could rule out a simple leak about the jewelry scam; it seemed likely the full circle of thespians involved in the ring knew about it. From what she'd heard from Lucas, Halloran, and O'Hara, Officer Nelson was an old friend of the Cleary family. No, the next victim would have to be involved on all fronts: as a connection to the MacDougal cabin and Little Tyrol, Wisconsin; as someone both beautiful enough to serve as an escort for the jewels and devious enough to fool everyone and keep her finger in all the pies. But now this woman's involvement would be her downfall.

Glenda pondered all this, and then remembered Chick's words: "Manzetti, in his sick obsessive way..."

With those words echoing in her mind, the cacophony of the nightclub disappeared; the loud talk and music seemed to die away. Suddenly the room went black. After a few catcalls and some nervous laughter, a spotlight illuminated the smiling specter from the night of Susan's murder, sitting at a shiny black upright piano on the left side of the small stage.

But the specter this time differed from the one she'd seen at the DePaul University practice rooms, the one she knew to have been Leo Cleary. He looked heavier, less lanky; his eyes seemed more piercing now and she could see in the spotlight that they were dark-circled and brown. It's Tony Manzetti, Glenda realized. Soon he broke into a snappy ragtime that she didn't recognize. But she could tell that Manzetti's playing lacked the sparkle of Leo Cleary's. Although his technique sounded firm, he played as if by rote; his style sounded stifled, forced, as if he were imitating without true feeling. He was like the empty piano in Little Tyrol filled with counterfeits, thought Glenda. Manzetti was an empty void trying to become whole through someone else.

He finished. The room applauded. He made several deep bows and grabbed the microphone from the stand. Glenda could smell the incense released through the air ducts.

"No, I'm not the ghost you're looking for," Manzetti said, smiling broadly. "He comes out when the spirit moves him. But let me introduce the next best thing — Cleary's own Leo Cleary!"

From the depths of the stage Leo Cleary emerged, his beard now almost fully grown back, his blue eyes twinkling. In his long-fingered hands he held a shiny golden soprano saxophone that resembled a clarinet. His shoulders relaxed as he blew life into the horn, his mouth assertive and forceful, his body movements fluid; it was a skilled dance of love with his instrument. Glenda thought how different he was from Manzetti, who had sounded so devoid of feeling, so cold and calculated.

Cleary was languid yet flowing full of passion. All at once, Cleary slid onto the piano seat, ended the slow sexy jazz number on his horn, and swept into the "Maple Leaf Rag," his hands practically flying off the keyboard as he raced from one octave to another.

Glenda knew there was no mistaking the original specter. It had definitely been Cleary who had played the role, bringing in business with his theatrical and musical talent. Despite her contempt for his flagrant womanizing, Glenda could still feel his undeniably powerful and sensuous charm. Then, amid this lustful reverie, she looked over at Jack, who was watching her with his all-accepting open smile.

Grinning, she started back toward his table. Thunderous applause erupted around her as Cleary left the stage. Looking up, just behind the side curtains at stage right, she saw the watchful eyes of Tony Manzetti. His face looked hard, ruthless, as he stared at Cleary.

Glenda followed his gaze to the table directly in front of the stage, where Pamela had risen to her feet and was clapping vigorously. What was he waiting for? Glenda wondered. Then Pamela Burke crumpled and collapsed to the floor.

Chapter Seventeen

P andemonium followed as a crowd formed around Pamela's crumpled figure, lying motionless on the lavender-scented floor.

Glenda acted quickly. Rushing to the bar phone, she dialed Detective O'Hara's number while confused bystanders gathered. Glenda could see just her stockinged legs splayed awkwardly, one black pump lying nearby.

Glenda had no address off the top of her head and simply told the police operator, "Cleary's Club, on Halsted near DePaul University. It's poison - hurry!" As she spoke, she watched as those who had not noticed Pamela's collapse danced to music playing over the house P.A. Others rushed to the fallen woman's side. Even from across the room, Glenda could see a look of deep concentration on the face of Monty Simms, the only unmoving figure in the swirl of activity around Pamela's body.

Soon paramedics arrived. Glenda's stomach turned for the parallels to the night of Susan's murder struck her dumb. Intellectually she knew this was a different situation, a different person — but it must be the same murderer.

Glenda swiftly crossed the room, hooked her arm in Monty's, and scooted him down a side corridor and into Cleary's dressing room.

"What is it, Glenda?" Monty demanded. "All hell's breaking loose out there and I've got to go back and deal with the police."

"That's right. What do you know about it? You looked preoccupied out there. I saw you carrying in the tuxedo tails before — so who are you helping in this scam? Leo or Manzetti? It's all over, Monty, so talk! Pamela could die."

"Pamela Burke?"

"Who do you think just passed out? Mama Cass?"

"Oh my God oh my God oh my God." Simms put both hands to his shaggy blond head as if trying to block out distracting noise.

"What is it, Monty?" Glenda clutched his sleeve. "You have to tell me! Two women have died. I failed Susan because I didn't see how deeply she was involved. But it's got to stop here! What are you holding back?"

Simms hesitated. "Your friend Susan gave me something, but it made no sense. She was nuts, you know. I think it was a gag."

Glenda grabbed his arm as he started to sit down."Don't touch anything. Detective O'Hara should be on his way."

As she said this, she noted everything in the room that might be important: an alto saxophone lying with its curved bell face up in an open case; Leo's leather bomber jacket draped over a chair; some sheet music; the glass of water Cleary soaked his reeds in. But for some reason it stood by the sink. Glenda recalled having seen it next to Cleary whenever he warmed up, placed on a small round table near the other corner of the room.

"Tell me first, Monty — doesn't Cleary usually soak his reeds over there, next to his chair?"

She pointed. Monty looked frazzled.

"I don't know. Yeah, I guess."

"Then why is the glass by the sink?"

"I don't follow you."

"Let's just say I think Detective O'Hara will find traces of poison on that glass. I have a theory about the women in Leo Cleary's life. But first — what did Susan give you?"

"It's in my office."

"I'll wait here."

He hesitated, as if afraid to tell her more.

"You know, Glenda, your friend Susan was a very confused woman. She drank too much too."

Glenda nodded. "Confused about Leo and Tony? If that's what you mean, then yes — I know she went back to Leo whenever he wanted. I heard in particular about the traditional pre-show warm-ups. It was a known fact that most of his women scrambled to test out Leo's horn for him before the shows."

Monty looked relieved.

"Then what I'm going to show you shouldn't surprise you."

Simms left the room and returned after several moments carrying a long cylindrical tube. Glenda recognized the manufacturer's name on the label but couldn't place the name "Fabray" right away. He handed it to her.

"What is it?" she said, opening the end.

"It's a roll. You know, like the upright Leo does his act on."

"Like a music roll for a player piano?" Glenda asked.

"Guess so. See, I told you your friend was nuts. I think it's a joke. She left it for me."

"She wasn't nuts," Glenda said, a slow grin crossing her face. "She knew exactly what she was doing. I have a player piano at home. Let's test it out. Only problem is, I don't know how to work it."

"Neither do I."

"Wait a minute...Lucas MacDougal! He'll know. As soon as O'Hara arrives, we're out of here."

An hour later Glenda, Lucas MacDougal, and Monty Simms stood around the player piano in her living room while Jack made popcorn in the kitchen. Lucas fumbled with the tab at the end of the roll before hitching it somewhere inside the front sliding door of the piano. Then, lifting the top open, he peered inside while adjusting a metal knob at the right-hand side of the instrument.

"I hope this old baby works," she said. "I've never tried a roll on it before."

With a flick of the switch, pumping sounds began. Then, all at once, the keys depressed on their own and plucked out music. As the middle and soprano octaves magically sang, seeming to exert their own will over the instrument, Glenda felt goosebumps form on her arms.

"That's the mysterious roll? What's that song?" wondered Monty. "I don't know it."

Lucas hummed along, tilting his head from side to side. A slow-moving tune, it sounded like a ballad or love song. Glenda jumped up from the piano bench suddenly.

"My God, I played that for a clarinet festival when I was a kid. It's 'My Wild Irish Rose'!"

Lucas nodded excitedly. "I remember now."

"So what's the message from Susan?" Monty said. "I don't get it?"

"Rose, Rose... Why would she give us this?" Glenda asked Monty. "Do you know where she got it?"

"She said she stole it from the Cleary mansion," responded Monty, "the big one in Pinehurst. When Leo got wind of it he was mad, but she still wouldn't tell him where she'd stashed it. Then the night she was murdered she gave me the roll just before show time and told me to keep it. I figured she was drunk."

"Looks like a motive for murder to me," remarked Jack, walking in with two large bowls of popcorn.

"The Pinehurst mansion, huh?" Glenda said, thoughtfully, hand to her chin. "And why do roses ring a bell? My God! The tapestry! I noticed it when you were talking to Chick, Lucas. Do you remember it?"

"Sort of," responded Lucas, vaguely. "The one in the living room?"

"Yes. It was hanging over the entrance to that gorgeous room filled with velvet chairs. Now I know why it struck me as interesting at the time. It was the same design as the one in the backdrop of that photo Jake stole from me in North Kenwood. You know? The one of the Six Dixies? Lucas, you told me he was afraid I'd make connections between the Clearys and the MacDougals and the Six Dixies, and that he was trying to protect the MacDougal name. But I think Johnny Cleary had bigger ideas. And that tapestry is filled with roses on its backdrop. But why the tapestry?"

Lucas smiled suddenly.

"What is it?" asked Glenda.

"I guess this is where my old age comes in handy. I distinctly remember the parties at the old Pinehurst mansion, and that tapestry was always hanging there. I don't know if that's significant. Then there was the beautiful Rose herself. She was always around, singing in that heavenly voice of hers."

"Let's hope someone's at the mansion now," Glenda said. "Jack, we're going out to the Pinehurst house. You and Lucas stay here and see if the hospital calls about Pamela's condition. I gave this number."

"Got it," Jack said. "You sure you know what you're doing?"

"I'm taking Monty with me. We'll be fine."

As they drove the fifteen minutes to neighboring Pinehurst, Glenda watched Monty from the side as they waited at a stoplight. He rubbed his hands together continually. She noticed he looked left and right as she drove and the streets transformed from homey and comfortable Rosedale into the opulent hilltops of Pinehurst.

Finally they turned down the leaf-strewn cul-de-sac where the Cleary mansion stood. As they neared the place, the sky itself seemed to darken and the treetops to close in overhead, bowing in the breeze. A single harsh light shot through an upstairs window of the mansion, shrouded in dying vines.

"How are we going to get in!" Monty said.

"She's home," Glenda said. "It won't be a problem."

Monty stopped fidgeting and fixed his gaze on her.

"Who's home?"

"She's been waiting a long time. Decades, in fact."

Minutes later they passed the two profile statues in front of the house and stood in the shadows of the front entranceway. Monty looked haunted — perhaps because of Glenda's words, or because of the overpowering force of the house itself. It somehow seemed to demand reverence to its grandeur. He felt young and scared, like a child playing trick-or-treat who'd stumbled upon the town ghoul's house by accident. Glenda too felt apprehensive, as if so much of the tragic mystery behind Susan's death depended on who or what would answer.

"No one's answering," he muttered nervously. "Let's get out of here."

As he spoke, the heavy mahogany door creaked open arthritically. The twinkling light from a chandelier blinded them momentarily. The person in the doorway stood like a stencil outline, an unknown entity.

"I was expecting you," an older woman's voice said. "I just wasn't sure when. I'd hoped it would be soon. Susan was worried no one would come. Of course, it's too late for her now."Her words were imbued with finality, like a slammed door.

"May we come in?" Glenda said, her heart pounding.

The petite woman, almost miniature, stepped back slowly. Despite her aged appearance, her pale blue eyes twinkled mischievously. It was Helen Moss, Lucas' sister.

As they entered the mansion, Glenda noticed Monty looked troubled. The house was overwhelming, exactly as Glenda remembered it, but this time all the antiques looked dusted and cared for, as if given new life.

"Please sit down."

"I'm afraid we don't have time," Glenda said. "Pamela Burke is in the hospital and may not make it. I'll get right to the point."

"You found the piano roll," Helen Moss said solemnly.

"How the hell d'you know that?" Monty said.

Glenda touched his arm. "Helen," she said, "we've met before, haven't we? At Northwestern's music library? You were the sixth member of the Six Dixies, right?"

She smiled. "Sorry to have deceived you, Glenda. I couldn't let you see me....I was just trying to protect the Cleary name. Susan, with her great determination and detective work, found the piano roll. Young Jake Cleary had stashed it without knowing what it was. He's in on the mob, you know, just like his great grandfather. The difference is that back in the old days, Johnny didn't like what was going on, and he revolted against Doc Reilly and Manzetti's family."

"Tony Manzetti's family?" Glenda asked.

"I expect so. You see, Jake MacDougal was worried about his family's involvement being found out. As far as I understand it, back in the old days when Johnny Cleary realized what was going on — the numbers, the illegal liquor racket, and the women — he and Siberius MacDougal were going to pull out of the deal. That's when Reilly and some unknown cohorts arranged the murder of Rose Green as a warning. Little did Reilly know that whoever it was would double-cross him and have Reilly himself also killed."

"And you were the only one with the inside knowledge, isn't that right?"

"Yes," Helen said quietly.

"Well," Monty broke in sarcastically. "What Leo does is, he plays dumb. Not to mention that he really *is* a drug addict. He's also far gone on the supernatural stuff."

"Well," Helen said. "Some of us believe in mediums and spiritual channels."

"Yeah," Monty countered, "but what Leo's doing is using the thrill of ghosts as a scare tactic to bring in business. He'd do anything to save the club. He closes his eyes to the illegal stuff, and pretends it's all in the Cleary's name."

"What I fear now," Helen said, "is that that's why the women involved in these tawdry activities are being killed."

"You gotta admire the guy for trying to keep the club going," Monty said.

Glenda turned on him. "Are you kidding? With drug dealing and murder? There are better ways to keep a business going. We're all feeling the recession. That doesn't mean we all become underhanded. Come clean, Monty. Tell us your involvement with Manzetti to overthrow Cleary in the business. I know all about it."

His eyes widened as he stepped back.

"You're nuts! You're as crazy as Susan was! No wonder you were friends."

Glenda changed her tactic suddenly. "Look," she said. "You wouldn't have given us the piano roll if you didn't want the insanity and the murders to stop. I think the roll is a clue to what happened during Prohibition. And it may map out ownership of the club, which is important to both Lucas and Jake. But the crucial point is that the past of the club, its ownership, and especially the murders in the nineteen-twenties, explain the murders now. I recognize the behavior of this killer. He's obsessed."

"'Obsessed?'" said Monty skeptically. "What the hell are you talking about?"

Glenda walked to the parlor and stood under the tapestry. She recalled now the frozen black and white faces of the Six Dixies as they'd sat, posing for the photograph she had found in the antique shop.

"Helen?" she said. "What do you think? What about this tapestry? What's the connection between it and Cleary's and the Six Dixies? I think whoever hung it here knew it once was a backdrop in Cleary's Club. And it's full of roses," she said, pointing to it. "See here, and here. There's got to be a connection to the piano roll and 'My Wild Irish Rose.'"

Helen followed her into the parlor. The two women formed a sharp contrast; Glenda's tall, brunette figure standing next to the hunched-over, eighty-something figure of Helen Moss. The two strolled around the room, examining the ceilings, the stenciled walls, and the black and white tiled floor. Then Glenda pointed to a fenced-in area out in the yard, overgrown with twisting ivy and moss.

"What's that?" she said.

The crystalline blue in Helen's eyes sparked brightly again.

"Of course!" Helen said, her voice youthful suddenly. "Why didn't I see it before? That's the original rose garden out back. That fenced-in area is where Mrs. Edith Cleary, Johnny's mother, used to grow her prize-winning roses every year for the Pinehurst festival. She was fiercely proud of her garden, from what I understand."

"So who would have known about that?" Glenda mused. "Johnny himself certainly. So maybe he's left some sort of message in the piano roll.... Or maybe he's *literally* left something in the rose garden for someone to find."

"Hope it's not a body," Monty said cynically.

As Glenda spoke, she strode through the French doors leading out to the sprawling lawn. After a moment, she turned back to Helen, her eyes imploring.

"I'm sorry. But we have to dig up your yard. I know it's practically hallowed ground, but I have a feeling the key to these three murders is buried somewhere out here."

Minutes later, while Monty paced and smoked and Helen Moss rested on a cast iron lawn chair, Glenda pushed back the rusted gate of the rose garden with a small shovel held in her hand.

Chapter Eighteen

As Glenda dug a six-foot ditch, red and brown dirt piled up around her and the sky tightened its austere hold on the sun, leaving splashes of purple and grey in its wake. Monty's nervousness grew, and he paced closer and closer to Glenda until he stood directly over her.

"Let me help for a while, or something," he said, half-heartedly.

Straightening, she handed him the shovel.

"You know," he said, "now that I think about it, a lot of women liked to hang around Leo's dressing room back stage before the shows, just like you described."

Glenda stretched and settled on a bench near Helen's lawn chair. She nodded.

"Well," she said, "if my suspicions are right, Susan and Pamela both tried out Leo's saxophone before the shows."

Monty exhaled. "That's true. I've seen 'em both do it. Used to piss Tony off to no end. I don't know if he was mad because they were in Leo's way, or if it was the flirting that made him mad."

"Yes," Glenda said, standing and pacing. "Let's think for a second what those two women, and Claudia Reinert, the strangled victim, have in common. Susan was an alcoholic — that much I know."

"Pam has a big thirst too," Monty said. "She's gotten herself into a few too many scrapes at the club as a result of drinking — over Leo or some other guy. I can vouch for that."

"Point one: they both drank a lot," Glenda said. "And both Susan and Pamela dated Leo Cleary at one time, then eventually dated Tony Manzetti. But what about Claudia?"

"Yeah, Susan and Pam dated both guys," Monty confirmed. "But I'll tell you. Manzetti always got real hot under the collar about his women. He was nuts about your friend Susan. Even though everybody knew he was seeing that Professor Carolyn person behind

Susan's back, he always acted real possessive of his girls. The Claudia girl? I don't know. All I know is that she was close to Leo."

"And all three women were involved in the counterfeit ring," Glenda said. "Two of the women, Susan and Claudia, were found wearing the earrings. Is there anything else you can tell me?"

Monty thought for a moment. "Let me see," he said. "I hate to tell you this, but I think Susan was on other stuff besides alcohol. She was hyper."

"Cocaine?"

"Maybe."

"Or speed," said Glenda, then snapped her fingers. "My God, she had hypertension. She suffered from it even back in college."

"Wouldn't she have been quite a young person for that ailment?" Helen asked.

"She had an uneven heart rhythm or something, too, I think. She had to go in and be tested every couple months. She really wasn't supposed to drink or do any drugs, but I know she was into speed and coke for a while. Anyone who knew her knew about her drug habits. Especially those people dealing in drugs, with a counterfeit jewelry scam as a front. What do you think, Monty? Why don't you come clean and tell the truth? Manzetti's your partner, isn't he?'

Monty stopped pacing and glared at her. Then his eyes dropped, avoiding Helen Moss's intense gaze.

"You'd take over Leo's club?" Helen asked, softly. "Take it away from him? Something that's been in his family for generations?"

"You don't know," Monty said, his voice hoarse. "You're just guessing."

Glenda shook her head. "I've seen Griz doing grunt work, running errands like picking up tuxedos for Manzetti. I've seen the fear Manzetti's instilled in everyone who knew him or worked for him. And he's very close to Leo — has been forever, since their college days."

"That's right!" Monty said with conviction. "So why would Manzetti want to double-cross Leo? Or me, for that matter?"

"Because you want to save the club, and Manzetti wanted it for himself. You're worried about Leo's stability, I could see that from the start. Jack filled me in on your plans for the club the night he met you. You needed a lot of income. But maybe Manzetti went too far. Manzetti knew Leo was out of control and he didn't want the added risk. He became obsessed."

Monty rubbed his forehead and turned away. When he looked back at the two women, observing Helen's sad bewilderment and Glenda's determined stare, his eyes were full.

"The guy got crazy! I don't know. Maybe the women drove him over the edge! You got it right. He was 'obsessed'! That's when I started to get worried."

"Worried for whom?"

"For the business, for the jewelry racket. The Wisconsin connection had been loyal to the Clearys for decades, but even Mack at the piano roll store up there questioned Manzetti's dealings. He went along with the jewelry stuff. But when Manzetti brought in the drugs, that's when I called it quits."

"When was that?"

"About a week ago. I said if he didn't clean it up, I was out. He acted like he didn't hear me. He just looked at me, like I hadn't said anything. And then he showed me the earrings."

Glenda started.

"Earrings? Were they cameo earrings? They looked like two statues and were black and white?"

"Yeah, how'd you know?"

"What did he say he was going to do with them?"

"That they were a gift for some very deserving young woman. He liked giving out those counterfeits lately, I don't know why. I told him he shouldn't be passing out the merchandise, you know, that the broads might wear 'em in public. And then he said the strangest thing. He said, 'it wouldn't be the first time someone would wear 'em for the last time.'"

Glenda felt a shiver run up the back of her neck. Her eyes smoldered. "'Wouldn't be the first time someone would wear them for the last time?'" she repeated. "Don't you see how significant that is?"

Monty frowned. "Why? The guy never makes sense! And talk about *possessive*. Man! The women he knew had to play it straight or pay the consequences."

"Pay the consequences? Like Susan and Claudia did? And now Pamela," Glenda mused, her eyes downcast.

Monty did a double take. "You think Manzetti's behind the murders?"

Glenda rose from the bench and took another small shovel Helen had just brought from a nearby shed. Monty stood back and wiped his brow.

"I need to get going," he said. "This is all too much. I doubt we'll find anything and I have things to do at the club."

Glenda and Helen watched him walk to his car parked at the side of the house. Then Glenda squatted by the hole they'd dug. Her face, even in the increasing darkness, was bright with excitement suddenly.

"Helen. Shine the flashlight here."

She poked at something in the ditch with her small shovel, scraping back dirt with her bare hands.

"I see something sleek and shiny. Lots of colors."

"What is it?" Helen said anxiously.

"I have to pull it out, hold on." Glenda reached in and lifted out an ornamental box.

"It looks like a jewelry case," Helen said.

"A very large jewelry case," Glenda said, wiping the top off with a corner of her blouse.

Glenda hopped out of the hole and they walked to the back patio where Helen had flipped on a light.

"Let's take a closer look under the light," she said.

Glenda sat on a wrought iron chair and opened the box. The hinges on the back snapped and the entire lid broke off.

"Here's a small book," Glenda said. "It says 'Diary of Rose Green.'" She handed it to Helen. "And here's some sort of log." She glanced at it quickly. "It seems to list shipments and money activities of Cleary's from," she flipped the pages, "1915 through 1929. My God, a lot of this isn't very upstanding. No surprise I guess. There's notes here about prostitution, names of local businessmen and politicians...gambling locations."

"And what's this," Helen said, sitting next to Glenda. "I recognize some of these names. These were local Chicago hoods. They were like liaisons with the bigger mobsters."

Glenda turned more pages. "Helen? Is this what I think it is?" she said, tracing names with her finger. "It says 'Terminate' at the top and Doc Reilly and Rose Green are on here. Is this a proverbial hit list?"

But Helen had grown silent. She'd opened another log from the lacquered box and now unfolded a piece of yellowed paper.

"What is it?" Glenda asked hurriedly.

"It's some sort of title. If I'm reading it right, it legally left Cleary's Club to...Angelo Manzetti."

Glenda turned to Helen. "May I use your phone?"

"Go ahead, dear — go inside and help yourself. It's next to the cherrywood rolltop desk."

Glenda found the telephone quickly. She dialed the Rosedale Community Hospital, her finger trembling in the old rotary dial.

"Yes, is there a patient there by the name of Pamela Burke? Or is Detective O'Hara there?"

A cordial receptionist rang the room. A coarse male voice answered at the other end.

"Hello?" The voice was gruff, suspicious.

Glenda knew that voice. Suddenly she couldn't speak.

"Tony?"

"Yes?"

She steadied herself. "It's Glenda. Is Detective O'Hara there?"

"How are you, Glenda?"

"Fine, Tony."

Slight hesitation. "Hold on."

"O'Hara here."

"Detective," Glenda whispered hurriedly, "watch Manzetti like a hawk! Don't answer my questions with him there. Did you remove a small water glass from the dressing room at Cleary's Club? If not, get it right away and check for traces of liquid amphetamines. If you did take it, check for prints too like you always do. But Detective, this is important — check Pamela's purse for a pair of cameo earrings. Dust them for prints, too. It might be enough to go on."

"I don't get any of what you're talking about."

"Don't talk about it now."

"Fine. Let's meet later."

Glenda hurried. "Call me at my house tonight. I'll arrange something. I can't discuss it with you now because he might hear you."

Glenda raced outside again. "Helen. Thanks for your help. I have to go. May I hold on to the box and its contents?"

She nodded, but her face looked troubled.

"What is it, Helen?"

"I should have told you earlier. I'm just so used to protecting Johnny. I don't know that it's important now but I think you should know. A woman, a farming widow, wrote to me from a post office box in Iowa around fifteen years ago. She said Johnny Cleary had sought refuge in their small town in the late thirties and had in fact spent his final years with her. He didn't die until 1983."

Glenda looked thoughtful. "That poor man. To live with all the blame of the murders all those years."

******

"Jake? It's Glenda Dominique. You have to meet us. I'm with Monty Simms. We need you to bring the photo of the Six Dixies. Detective O'Hara will be there too."

"Why are you still after that damn picture?" said Jake, impatiently.

"Helen Moss told me the band members are listed on a sheet hidden in the back of the old frame."

"So what? So we find out who's in the band. I can tell you that already."

"Look, Jake. Original ownership rights of Cleary's Club were divided up among the first three members, right?"

"Right. And they were Johnny Cleary, the piano player; Doc Reilly, the other keyboard man; and Tommy Smythe, the clarinet player. What else could you need to know?"

"That picture in particular is the earliest one we know of. Even the Music Library at Northwestern didn't have one that old. I think the original three band members were different than we thought. Please, just meet me tonight with the picture."

He sighed. "Fine. Where?"

She thought a moment. "The safest place I can think of is out front of the hospital. That way we'll be close to Pamela — just in case."

"In case what?" Jake said, his voice tight.

"She's in danger, Jake. Pamela could die. She may have been slipped some poison, like the other victims."

Long pause. "I thought she just drank too much. The doctors said they were worried about her heart, but they didn't know exactly what was wrong. Are you telling me she was poisoned like Susan?"

"Probably. And in the same way, I think. The difference was that Susan had hypertension, and whoever murdered her knew it."

"Oh my God," Jake said suddenly.

"What?"

"Pamela just found out last year she has a weak heart. She was adopted, so up until then she didn't know much about her family tree. This came as a big shock. But you know how she is with booze, and she wouldn't give up the other drugs either."

"What other drugs?"

"Speed. Black beauties, she calls them."

"Did you tell the doctor about all this?"

"Yes."

"Good. We don't have any time to waste. Meet us with the photo at eleven tonight. Can you do it?"

At ten-thirty that night, Glenda and Monty waited for Detective O'Hara and Jake MacDougal to arrive. Monty paced incessantly. Glenda frowned as he lit another cigarette. The chill night air intimated winter's definitive arrival. The once yellow maple trees around the hospital grounds now seemed to shiver nakedly like the skeletons of bygone summers.

"So Monty," Glenda said, hugging herself in the cold. "Tell me something. We know why Jeremiah and Johnny Cleary got into the mob dealings during the Depression, but why did Leo get involved again now? Was the club so important?"

Monty kicked the ground with the toe of his expensive loafers. He looked disgusted. "Leo's always been unbalanced," he scoffed. "He's so damn theatrical! He's made his music a sideshow. But he's a pothead and God knows what else. Seems like everyone in the music business either does drugs and booze, or they're recovering addicts. The curse of the creative types, right?" He stopped a moment, re-lit his cigarette with shaky hand, and continued. "A while back, Manzetti started spreading rumors that Leo was really unbalanced and couldn't cut it as a partner in the club. Manzetti came up with a plan to take over the club once the hauntings and the drugs and all brought in enough income to clear the debt. He was going to have Leo proved legally incompetent — to the benefit of the other partners."

"Quite a plan," Glenda said.

"The only problem was, Manzetti was utterly ruthless. He'd have done anything. He's the one who got all the girls, the theater friends of Leo's, mixed up in the escort shit."

Glenda nodded, deep in thought. "Frankly, I thought I knew Susan better," she said. "She was wild in college but she seemed unbothered by things. Her parents never had much money so I know that making it into a sorority was important to her. She wanted the brass ring and she'd do anything to get it."

"Manzetti would do anything too," Monty said. "Even illegal

stuff. I got nervous. Miranda and I got into a yelling match over it out front of that high-priced antique store in North Kenwood, — you know, the day you and Jake were both trying to buy the photograph of the Six Dixies? Miranda was trying to defend Griz to me. She kept telling me that whatever information Susan gave me would somehow get Griz in trouble. She didn't even know what it was. I told her I believed it would actually tell us more about the club — its rightful ownership and all. To tell you the truth, I figured it'd tell us even more than that."

"Like what?" Glenda said.

"Well, there was talk that ownership of the place was in doubt. Leo Cleary didn't inherit it straight out — old Johnny had lost it in a poker match. The place was due to be torn down in the nineteen-seventies. It had been a shambles for years and was now owned by a holding company. So no one really knew who owned it after its heyday and the scandal of the murders back in the twenties."

"Monty, why are you telling me all this now?"

"Because I realized Manzetti was getting nuts. For a long time I suspected that either Cleary or Manzetti was unstable. It didn't hit me that they'd be connected with the murders until I saw how power-hungry Manzetti was."

"Not only that," Glenda added. "Did you know that he played the specter the night of Susan's murder?"

"No wonder," Monty said.

"What?"

"He had me show Jack around outside that night at around two a.m. You know, supposedly to explain our plans for expansion."

"Interesting."

Monty nodded nervously. "Like I said, he'd do anything to get what he wanted. But then all the women he knew started dropping dead."

"And why is it," asked Glenda, "that all the women entangled with Manzetti were once involved with Leo Cleary? I think Manzetti's obsessed with Leo. He's always acted like his best friend ever since their roommate days back in college. But I think somewhere he crossed the fine line between sanity and insanity. He's aimed for and achieved every goal, every woman, and now every business venture that Leo Cleary has ever been involved in. And Leo himself just seems to be getting more and more out of touch with reality. It could be his pot smoking or just mental imbalance."

"I'll tell you, Manzetti's been counting on that," Monty said.

"That's not all Manzetti was counting on," Glenda commented, slyly.

Monty looked at her. "What do you mean?"

From under her corduroy jacket, Glenda pulled out a well-varnished jewelry case. Monty eyed it suspiciously.

"Where'd you get that?"

"After I called the hospital and you left for the club, Helen Moss and I discovered what Johnny Cleary must have hidden over seventy years ago. He desperately wanted someone from the Cleary clan to find it."

"I don't get it. Who did he leave the piano roll to? Before Leo got hold of it?"

"Leo Cleary inherited the piano roll. Helen Moss was left the tapestry — with strict instructions, hand-written by Johnny, about where it should hang. I guess he hoped someone would figure it out."

Monty frowned. "Why leave such a vague message? Wasn't it kind of a long shot?"

"Sure. But that's all he could do; the mob was on to him. He knew all about the murders from Helen Moss — she went into hiding as well. What's in the box are not only Rose Green's diary, but a log showing all the shipping and payment activities of the Cleary operation from 1922 through 1929. It documents all the bootlegging, prostitution, and gambling — including the identities of all those involved with the Mafia. What's more, it reveals who was responsible for the hits on Doc Reilly and Rose Green. It also left the club legally in the ownership of the same person."

"Well, who the hell was it?"

"You won't believe it," answered Glenda, her voice low. "*Angelo Manzetti.* I have a feeling Tony knows that, and was trying to find these legal papers to prove the club belonged rightfully to him."

"So Johnny Cleary didn't murder those two after all? What happened to him, then?"

"He disappeared. According to Helen Moss, another woman he'd been involved with up until twelve years ago wrote to Helen in nineteen eighty-three and told her Johnny Cleary had died in a farming accident. Apparently he'd been hiding out in the wilderness of Iowa."

"Can you beat that?" Monty said, just as a tired-looking woman in a white lab coat hurried past.

"I'm sure the open air was enough to put him over the edge," Glenda mused. "He was a musician, and a city man by nature."

"I don't get it," he said, "Manzetti was sure that Cleary's rightfully belonged to us. He wanted to buy out any other partners, and said it was Cleary who was nuts. He said that insanity ran in the family. Angelo, his grandfather, pounded it into his head for years and years that the Cleary family was slime. In fact, he said it was Johnny Cleary who'd been mixed up with the Mafia."

Glenda nodded. "It was the opposite," she said over her shoulder as they walked down the corridor. "According to the records buried in Helen's garden, Angelo Manzetti was responsible for all the murders back then. He called the mob to do his dirty work whenever anyone crossed him or went against what he imagined were the interests of the club. Eventually he was shot to death in the basement of the club by his wife, who caught him with a hooker. He did a number on Tony Manzetti though.... My God, we *have* to get there in time!"

Then she looked at her watch. "Where are Jake and Detective O'Hara? Excuse me," she said, stopping a young woman in nurses' uniform who'd just walked behind the desk. "Has anyone named Jake MacDougal checked in at the late desk?"

"Jake MacDougal? I think I recall the name," she said, massaging her temples and pulling up the sleeves on her white cardigan. "We just let in a Jake MacDougal to see a patient upstairs, even though it's past visiting hours. But he was family and she'd been asking for him all night. He's a step-brother or something."

Glenda's heart jumped. Something didn't feel right. "What did he look like?"

"You know, nice-looking; dark hair and eyes," she said, smiling coyly.

"My God," Glenda said, pushing past the startled woman.

They took the stairs two at a time, Monty talking to Glenda's back as they ran.

"It's not Jake is it?" he said. "My God what if we're too late!"

They rushed down the dim hallways of the hospital. Here and there they passed a darkened doorway, where an empty bed and an open door indicated death or recovery. They passed two nurses speaking in hushed tones. One grabbed Monty's arm.

"It's late. How did you two get in here?"

"This is an emergency," Glenda said, pushing her out of the way without slowing down. As the two nurses stared after them, Monty shrugged, then ran after Glenda. Soon they came to the nurses' station and Glenda called to a woman behind the desk.

"Where's Pamela Burke's room? She's a new arrival. It's an emergency." Leaning over the desk she whispered to the nurse, "There's a dark-haired man posing as someone else. He's murdered two women already. Tell us where her room is or she'll be next!"

Seconds later the trio charged into a room at the end of the hall where Pamela Burke lay, pale and vulnerable. A dark figure leaned over her, hypodermic needle in his hand.

On the floor lay Jake MacDougal, the oval frame with the photo of the Six Dixies shattered on the floor nearby. Detective O'Hara was tied to a hospital chair.

Without hesitating, Glenda threw herself across the bed and rolled into Tony Manzetti, knocking him against the glass of the far window so hard that it shattered. He grabbed his shoulder, wincing in pain.

"Call a doctor," Glenda said, rising from the floor and bracing herself to kick him as Manzetti stood up again. "Did you inject her?" she demanded.

He smiled his dark, psychotic smile, his eyes brazen and empty.

"Wait and find out. Angelo's been preparing me for this moment for thirty-five years."

"Your grandfather was wrong. He lied to you. You've been brainwashed, Tony."

He lunged for her. "You're lying. Who are you anyway? You're a nobody. I'm a Manzetti! Our family *ran* Chicago in the twenties. We had it all before the Clearys finally dirtied it with their women and their gambling. The Manzettis had class. We knew all the right people from Lake Woods and the north side of the city. Louis Armstrong and Al Jolson knew Angelo Manzetti. They came to Cleary's to socialize with *my* family. Noel Coward talked to my grandfather when he worked on a script. Martha Graham danced with Angelo in the ballroom of the Cleary mansion in Pinehurst. My family was American royalty! You're nothing but common stock. You're not a Manzetti!" His voice grew hysterical. "It's the men and women like you who try to become a Cleary or a Manzetti by hanging around greatness. You really think your association with Leo could make you one of us? One of the chosen? A genius?"

Monty stifled a laugh. "Come off it, Tony! The Manzettis were dirt poor! They hung around the Clearys that was all!"

Glenda grabbed Monty's sleeve.

"I'm sure your family knew a lot of people," she said quickly, reassuringly. "And you found the original list of band members behind the photo didn't you? The one Jake brought? It listed the three original members who were the owners of Cleary's. It was Johnny Cleary, Rose Green and Doc Reilly, wasn't it?"

"Yeah," Tony sneered. "But Angelo took care of them, didn't he? But I couldn't find the legal document I wanted at the Pinehurst mansion."

"Then you can't claim the club," Monty said, defiantly.

Suddenly Tony's angry countenance took on a missionary fervor. "Edward Hopper got advice from my grandmother in much of his work. He got his inspiration for the painting 'Lighthouse Hill' from a trip he took with our family."

"Wait just a damn minute! I don't see how that can be..." Monty started again, until Glenda dug her heel into his foot.

"Intellectuals and artists are indeed attracted to each other," soothed Glenda.

Manzetti's eyes softened in the half light. Pamela stirred on the bed and coughed several times. In the welter of emotions, fraught with tension and hostility, no one spoke for several moments.

"And Greta?" Glenda asked, simply.

"Greta?" Monty said, cynically.

Glenda kicked him. Manzetti looked caught off guard, then returned to his reverie.

"Yes, the great Garbo," he said, distantly. "She was exquisite. Angelo knew her intimately, of course."

"Of course."

"He understands women. All the Manzetti men do. That's why women leave the Cleary men and come to us. They know what's good for them."

"Of course," Glenda said, backing up to the telephone on the bedside table, step by quiet step. "I'm amazed at your medical knowledge too," Glenda said, lowering her voice. "Tell me, how did you know that liquid amphetamine — given their history of high blood pressure — would work so effectively on Susan and Pamela?"

As Glenda spoke, she groped behind her back. Manzetti's clenched fists relaxed. "Angelo's brother, my great-uncle Mario, was a surgeon. I studied his medical journals. We spent a lot of time at his house in Lake Woods when I was growing up. Yes, Grandma Maria loved to rub it in how successful Mario was — always holding it over Angelo. 'Mario graduated from Northwestern, Angelo. What have *you* ever done?'" she'd say. 'Nothing but that club and gambling and women.'"

Then Manzetti's tone changed as he drew a revolver from the folds of his overcoat and stalked over to her. Monty Simms sidestepped quickly toward him but Glenda waved him back. "Why are you so interested?" he blurted angrily. "You're just a damn *woman*. What do you know?"

As he closed in on her Glenda counted over nine buttons on the touch-tone phone as if reading Braille and punched 9, then groped over and up to hit the number 1 twice. She quickly pressed the receiver against the back of her skirt so the operator's voice would be muffled.

"Monty?" she said, turning to him. "Didn't you say just yesterday that Leo wanted to get rid of his share of the club?"

Manzetti stopped abruptly. "What are you talking about?" he said.

Monty watched Glenda carefully, finally detecting the desperate urgency in her eyes.

"Yeah," he said eagerly, "that's what he told me when we went out for drinks in Pinehurst the other night. Right after he showed me the stuff at the mansion."

Manzetti turned to him, waving the gun wildly. "That can't be. I have the original earrings! Angelo designed them, you know. We Manzettis had all the talent too. We knew all the important people. Even though the whores never stopped bothering my Angelo. And now look what they've done to me!"

The windows rattled from the gusts off Lake Michigan. Cold seeped through the shattered glass where Manzetti had crashed into it. Glenda's hand felt cold and clammy on the receiver pressed against her skirt, yet sweat ran down the side of her face.

"That damn Leo," Manzetti muttered.

"What's that?"

They all turned. Leo Cleary stood in the doorway, recognizable despite the Johnny Cleary specter garb he still wore, straight from the club.

"What is it, man?" he said coolly to Manzetti. "What's happened to you?"

Glenda jumped in quickly.

"Tony was just telling us about the history of the Clearys and the Manzettis. The families have been friendly a long time, haven't they? I'm afraid the women always go for the Manzetti men though — right, Leo?"

She smiled widely, her eyes intense. Leo staggered in, oblivious to Glenda. She could hear the crunch of the lavender grains from the club under his shoes. He headed for Manzetti awkwardly, his arms out. Glenda thought he was moving much too abruptly. Manzetti raised the gun.

"You gave your usual flawless performance tonight, huh, Leo?" Manzetti raged. "Brought down the damn house?"

"Tony!" Glenda said, sharply. "You've got it all wrong. I majored in music for a while; I know about these things. You sounded far better than Leo tonight — your technique, your style. No wonder women prefer Manzetti men. Leo has nothing on you."

As she spoke, she slipped the receiver under the bedcovers to Pamela, who'd tugged on Glenda's blouse during the charade. Pamela shoved it under the pillow, trying to feign semi-consciousness as she did so. Glenda realized she needed a distraction, and reached for Pamela's purse.

"What's with you, Tony?" Leo said, savagely. "You were in on the counterfeit scheme right along with me! We were going to be partners in the club, just like we planned."

Glenda quickly withdrew one of the earrings from Pamela's bag. "Why these, Tony?" she asked, holding up a black and white cameo. "Why did you give your women these before killing them?"

The room froze. Tony looked stricken. Leo looked baffled.

"I gave them to deserving women only, like Susan and Pamela.... They both started out looking wealthy, you know, a sorority girl and a MacDougal daughter, but then I got to know them and they're nothing but common trash! Susan's family had nothing and Pamela wasn't a real MacDougal. She didn't grow up in affluent society like I thought. They were both counterfeits! So that's what I gave them — fakes for fakes!"

Glenda nodded, pretending to be sympathetic. She watched Tony Manzetti closely. "Disgusting how some people are, isn't it?" she said.

"You saw me in my tuxedo at the Pinehurst mansion. I set the stage with the granules and all to scare you all off and then Chick failed to get rid of that old fool Lucas. And that Claudia bitch was wearing the earrings the night of the party to torment me," he went on. "She threatened to tell everyone she knew about the jewelry scam; she was going to go to the police. I *had* to stop her. And the pathetic Pamela thought I was a ghost at the party in North Kenwood. I was being Johnny Cleary. It was easy to change from shorts and sandals into that tuxedo, murder Claudia and slip back into the party. And then Griz messed up Pamela that same night, which worked out perfectly for me. He was angry because she wanted out of the racket.... Griz would do anything for me. He fears me," smiled Tony eerily. "As he should."

Leo leaned forward, holding his head in his hands as if it throbbed. Overwhelmed, he looked up at last, his eyebrows knit in consternation. Glenda remained frozen, hoping the police would respond promptly to her 911 call. All at once the sound of Manzetti's gun being cocked broke through the silence — followed suddenly by Detective Halloran bursting into the room, and two police officers. Manzetti stood by, stunned, then set the gun on the floor with excessive calm. Minutes later, after Manzetti had been taken away, Jake was revived and Detective O'Hara was untied. He pointed to the water glass next to the bed.

"That reminds me," he said. "How did you know it was liquid amphetamines?"

"I'm a musician and a reed player myself; I realized that Leo must have been soaking his reeds before each performance," Glenda said. "Tony knew that too, but he also knew that Leo never used a new reed on the same night. He soaked them the night before, and performed with a broken-in reed — one which he'd already have set aside in his saxophone case. That's why Cleary had a reed in his mouth that first night I saw him backstage. He'd leave out the reeds in the glass for the girls, to let them think he'd be using them that night. So the women would unknowingly warm up on the saxophone reeds which had been soaking in the amphetamine-filled glass by his side. He never used those reeds. They were for show, like a treat for the girls. Only Tony, who'd been his roommate in music school, knew that Leo's method was to slap on his broken-in reeds from the previous night just before going on stage. No musician would let an amateur mess with a reed he was just about to use. Tony knew that."

"Well, thanks to your nine-one-one call," Detective Halloran said, "we at least knew that *something* was up when the trace came out to Rosedale General."

They walked out of the room once the nurse had seen to Pamela and stabilized her. As they rode down in the elevator, Detective O'Hara laughed lightly as he reviewed his notes from the crime scene at the club.

"What is it?" Glenda said, closing her eyes with a sigh.

"Funny thing," he said. "The street name for amphetamines is 'roses.' Get it? The Rose Green woman dies seventy years ago, then the rose tapestry thing and finally the clues in the rose garden?"

Glenda looked at him, a bit aghast. "Right," she said. "It's hilarious."

Kathleen Anne Fleming grew up in Illinois, reading Nancy Drew voraciously as a child. She wrote her first story when she was eight years old and graduated from DePaul University with a deree in English/Communications and is a member of Mystery Writers of America. Ms. Fleming has published numerous short stories, including a collection, *One Impulsive Black Rose,* and lives in Illinois with her family.